FADE
TO
BLACK

FADE TO BLACK

Alex Flinn

HarperTempest
An Imprint of HarperCollins*Publishers*

For Toni Markiet,
an editor in a million.
I am so glad my manuscript landed on your desk!

www.harpertempest.com

Library of Congress Cataloging-in-Publication Data
Flinn, Alex.
    Fade to black / Alex Flinn. — 1st ed.
        p.   cm.
    Summary: An HIV-positive high school student hospitalized
after being attacked, the bigot accused of the crime, and the
only witness, a classmate with Down Syndrome, reveal how the
assault has changed their lives as they tell of its aftermath.
    ISBN 0-06-056839-9 — ISBN 0-06-056841-0 (lib. bdg.)
    [1. Toleration—Fiction.   2. Hate crimes—Fiction.   3. HIV
(Viruses)—Fiction.   4. Down syndrome—Fiction.   5. High
schools—Fiction.   6. Schools—Fiction.]   I. Title.
PZ7.F6395Fa 2005   2004014506
[Fic]—dc22

Typography by Ali Smith
1   2   3   4   5   6   7   8   9   10
❖
First Edition

ACKNOWLEDGMENTS

The author would like to thank her family for their support, and the following persons for their invaluable help with this book:

Stacie Murray, Terry Link, Mary Mettis, and Loretta Etienne, all of AIDS Project Florida, for their guidance and fact checking; Pat Gladieux, Kersten Hamilton, and Lucille Shulklapper for various help with poetry, Down Syndrome, and Down Syndrome as poetry; George Nicholson, Paul Rodeen, Laurie Friedman, Marjetta Geerling, Catherine Onder, Meghan Dietsche, and Phoebe Yeh for help with this manuscript.

Special thanks to Barbara Brooks Wallace, writer and apparent Spanish scholar, for the poem which precedes this volume.

As always, a thousand thanks to my mentor and good friend, Joyce Sweeney. You are the best!

Y es que en el mundo traidor
nada hay verdad ni mentira:
todo es según el color
del cristal con que se mira.

RAMON DE CAMPOAMOR
(1817–1901)

And it is that in the treasonous world
nothing is truth nor lie:
everything is according to the color
of the crystal through which it is seen.

RAMON DE CAMPOAMOR
(1817–1901)

Pinedale Senior High School
"Home of the Panthers"
PINEDALE, FLORIDA

TO: Eugene Runnels, Principal
FROM: Celia Velez, Assistant
DATE: October 27
RE: Incident Involving HIV-positive Student

Alejandro Crusan, a junior, was apparently attacked this morning at the corner of East Main and Salem Court. According to his parents, Alex was en route to Dunkin' Donuts at 35 East Main at approximately 6:00 a.m. A witness, Daria Bickell, a special education (Down Syndrome) student at Pinedale, saw Alex's red SUV stopped at a red light. An assailant, said to be wearing a blue Pinedale Panthers letter jacket and carrying a baseball bat, attacked Alex's car, smashing the front windshield and passenger-side windows. When the assailant attempted to run around to the driver's side, Alex was able to drive away. The witness saw Pinedale student Clinton Cole, 16, leaving the scene.

Although this incident did not take place on school property, I have contacted the school board, and they have pledged full cooperation with local police. Due to the nature of the incident, and also Alex's HIV-positive status, police will investigate the incident under the Florida Hate Crimes statute.

1

Monday, 10:50 a.m., Principal Runnels's office,
Pinedale High School

CLINTON

How do they know I did it?

They ought to give me a stinking medal. If you asked most people around here "off the record," they'd agree with what I did. I mean, sure everybody wants to be politically correct—whatever that's supposed to mean. Just because Pinedale's a cow town doesn't mean we're all rednecks without opposable thumbs, no matter what people from Miami might think. But people move here because it's a safe place. Or it was. No one wants to die. All the political correctness in the world's not worth that.

And most people would agree with that, "off the record."

But on the record, there's this little problem: they can't. That's why my butt's here in a green plastic chair in Principal Runnels's office instead of a plain old wooden chair in English class where it belongs.

I've been here an hour now, since they called me out of third period. And Runny-nose is nowhere to be found. His secretary, Miss Velez, acts like he's out on some kind of top-secret school business. But I know better. The one time, I got caught with Brett and Mo in that now-notorious mascot-swiping incident—he was late then, too. When he finally showed up, he was carting groceries—eggs and milk and Chips Ahoy. You'd think a big important principal would get his wife to do the shopping. But you'd be wrong. The man is PW, and if you don't know what that means, check with me sometime when I'm in a better mood and I'll tell you.

Miss Velez walks by, trying to look casual. But I'm pretty sure she's checking to make sure I haven't bolted. I stand when she comes in the room (my daddy taught me right) and say in my politest voice, "Excuse me, Ms. Velez?" She wants to be called *Ms.*

"Yes, Clinton?"

"Um, I was thinking if Principal Runnels won't be here for a while, could I maybe go back to class? We've got a test in English, and I sure do hate to miss it."

Or, more important, I hate to miss Alyssa Black. She has that class with me. Other girls, if they're pretty, I get tongue-tied. But Alyssa's different in the way she looks at me. It's not just that she's got beautiful eyes. But she sees me different, I feel like. Other girls see a big jock who runs with the pack. With Alyssa, it's like she . . . I don't know, understands me, maybe. Is that corny? It's like she can see inside to the part that's still this little fat kid no one likes much, the part I try to hide from most people. Today's the day I was planning on asking her to homecoming. It'll put a big dent in my plans if she knows I'm in here or if I get detention. Alyssa doesn't hang with delinquents.

Miss Velez glances at the clock. When she looks back, her face is sort of hard.

"No, Clinton, you can't go to class. They'll be with you in a few minutes."

She's gone before I get the chance to ask who "they" are.

Figures she'd be against me. Alex—the guy this is all about—he's a spic like she is. Or *Latino* as my mother would say. My father says those kinds of people always stick together. "That's the problem with 'em," he'd say. "With the whole damn State of Florida, really. You work a job your whole life, then some spic fires you and hires his second cousin. It started down in Miami, but darned if it isn't spreading up north. And soon, it'll be the last American in Florida, heading out and taking the flag with him."

My father ought to know because that's what happened to him. The getting fired part. My father was one of the most powerful men in Pinedale. But when he lost his job, my mother left him. She said it was because she couldn't stand being around his "attitudes"—whatever that means—but Dad says different. He got a new job out of state, and now I hardly see him. Mom won't let me call him much either, on account of the cost of long distance and all the child support Dad *isn't* paying. Dad

4

can't really afford to call us, either. Mom would say that's a good thing. But I miss him.

My mom and I don't see eye to eye on much. She's sort of liberal, which is really what started this whole problem with the Crusans. She's always worrying about people's rights and so forth. When my little sister, Melody, started playing with Carolina Crusan at school, Mom said fine. Then Carolina invited Melody to sleep over their house. Mom said fine again. Go. Never mind that her HIV brother's going to unleash the black plague on Pinedale, Florida. Never mind that we don't know what type of germs and spores and junk is flying around their house (I always try not to breathe too much when I'm in class with him). Just go. Have fun. I tried to tell Melody not to eat anything over there and to wash her hands and not touch any sharp objects and not drink out of the glasses (was that really unreasonable?). But Mom made me shut up. "Stop scaring her, Clinton. She might say something to the Crusans." Like she's more worried about their feelings than her own daughter's safety.

That's when I realized I needed to take matters into my own hands. With Dad gone and Mom acting sort of crazy, what choice did I have? But I wasn't going to hurt the guy or nothing. I just wanted to scare him so he'd go back where he came from before anyone got hurt. I only wanted to protect my family, like my father would've.

Mom thinks I should feel sorry for Crusan, on account of he's got AIDS. Maybe I would feel bad for him if he was living in some other town where it didn't affect me or my family, or even if he just stayed home. Or even if he didn't sit by me in two classes, for that matter, and act like *we're* a bunch of hicks. I thought about asking Mom to take us out of Pinedale. Some kids' parents did that. They let them study at home. But Mom would've said no way. She's like that. Dad would've been different. Dad would've understood.

Miss Velez shows up again. She's smiling this time, so I guess Runny-nose must've finished buying the toilet paper and made it to work. She turns back to the door.

"Right this way, gentlemen."

I look back and see it's not Runnels following her.

Hey, what are the cops doing here?

Monday, 10:50 a.m., hallway during passing period,
Pinedale High School

DARIA

> *Maybe*
> *I am*
> *a ghost*
> *people look through*
> *like water.*
>
> *Maybe*
> *I*
> *am invisible*
> *so they do not*
> *know I watch.*
>
> *Maybe they*
> *think words*
> *are invisible*
> *so I cannot*
> *hear*
> *retard, retard, retard.*

7

But words are not
invisible.
Me either.
And I always,
always
watch.

ALEX

My mother's crying. I make out shapes . . . IV pole, television set, window. Hospital window with flowers on the windowsill. I shut my eyes quick. Mom can't know I'm awake. My face aches a little, and the rest of me feels like it's still asleep. Like, numb. Even closing my eyes hurts, but I keep them shut tight anyway. I'm not ready to talk to anyone and, what's more, I'm not sure I can. I can't even believe this has happened, so how can I talk about it?

And my mother's crying. Again.

Last year, when I was first diagnosed with HIV, my mother cried a lot. When she finally stopped crying, my parents took me to Disney World. It was pretty cool. Even though we lived in Miami, we hadn't been in years because my sister, Carolina—who's nine, now, eight years younger than I am—had been too young to go on many rides before that. I didn't think about why we went, that I was like one of those Make-A-Wish foundation kids who wants to see Mickey before he dies. It hadn't totally sunk in yet, you know?

Even though I felt fine, Mom made me ride in this

9

wheelchair we rented. In a stroke of brain dead-itude, I went along with it. There were tons of gimpy kids there, and we got to go right to the front at every ride. The line for Space Mountain was, like, two hours, but we shot up front and I stepped out of my wheelchair and got on. When the Disney guy let us ahead of this one family that was waiting, the dad turned to his son and said, "Don't you hate people like that—rent a wheelchair just to go first."

Mom started crying then, too. She yelled at the guy, "You should thank God you have healthy children. My son has HIV. He's dying." And all around, people who'd been happy and smiling started looking afraid or away. It ruined the whole trip.

That was the first time it really sank in that I was going to die. Me. Die.

Die.

We haven't gone back to Disney since then and, if I did, I wouldn't ride in a stinking wheelchair. I don't need one. I'm no poster boy, and I am nowhere near needing to see Mickey. Besides, they're making some big gains in AIDS medications. I could live twenty years, maybe. Maybe longer.

Or maybe not.

I don't have AIDS yet, anyway—that's the first thing anyone needs to know about me. I read all these books about it, and I know all about T-cell counts and viral loads, but the bottom line is: I was diagnosed with HIV a year ago, and I still feel fine. I'm not on meds yet. I'm hanging in, living with it. My doctors say if I keep doing what I'm supposed to, maybe they'll find a cure before I even get really sick.

So this year we didn't go to Disney. In August, before we moved here to Podunkville, Florida, we went to New York City, and my mom and Aunt Maria took me to see this Broadway play called *Rent*. It won a lot of awards, and it's about people with AIDS. Of course, of all the musicals in New York, we had to see the one about AIDS. The people in the play, they're all junkies and homosexuals, and they're dealing with the fact that they're going to die, like, tomorrow. Aunt Maria hated the show because 1) It had loud music with electric guitars and stuff, which interfered with her sleeping; 2) It was depressing; 3) She said, "None of these people are like you, Alejandro. You are an innocent victim." I guess she meant because the people in the show were in what you'd call high-risk categories. Still, I think everyone with AIDS is an innocent victim. Most of the people I've met with HIV *are* in those higher-risk categories, and who cares? I don't think anyone deserves to get sick or die. I mean, I wouldn't wish this disease on Clinton Cole, much less some innocent homosexual.

Clinton Cole is what DC Comics would call my nemesis. He's Joker to my Batman, Green Goblin to my Spidey. Since we moved to Pinedale, people have pretty much been assholes. But Clinton's, like, the uber-asshole.

11

The first weeks of school, it seemed like any time I turned a corner, everyone dove together, whispering. Did they think that because they were whispering, I didn't know they were talking about me? And the people who don't whisper walk right past you in the hall, looking down, pretending not to see you. I try not to get mad at those people, because I remember I used to do it myself before. When you see someone in a wheel-chair or missing a leg or something, you don't want to seem like you're staring, so you look away. Which I now know is worse. And a lot of people backed up close to the wall when I walked by. The up side (if you'd call it that) was, I didn't have any trouble getting through the halls because no one would touch me.

But then there were the people like Clinton. People who didn't care what I heard or thought. When I walked into the cafeteria the second day, he stood up and said, "Go back where you came from, fag." And you could tell everyone was with him. Since then he's been doing all kinds of other crap. He wore a surgical mask one day to Government because we sit next to each other. I think he's one of the people who left threatening notes in my locker, though I don't know for sure.

We moved here for Dad's job. We'd lived in Miami all my life, and it wasn't perfect, but it was better. I had some friends, like Austin and Danny, and other guys I hung with at school. Sure, a few people were weird, but not as many. And even though I stopped playing baseball when

I got diagnosed, I was on the debate team. I made it to State with my original oratory last year, and I was going to try again this year.

Then Dad's company wanted to start an office here in Pinedale (Why here? Hell if I know), and they transferred him. I knew my parents didn't want to live here in the sticks, where there isn't so much as a Target, much less a mall. We have to drive to Gainesville to find a doctor who knows how to deal with me, and there are for sure no AIDS centers here. Without me, my parents probably wouldn't have come here. They'd have choices. Dad could get a different job. But Dad had to stay with the company to keep his health insurance. We're pretty much uninsurable as new patients because of me.

And you know what the debate team at Pinedale is? Two guys who gave me the evil eye when I walked through the door. I walked right back out. It's not even worth trying to make friends in Pinedale.

And now I'm here in the hospital, listening to my mother crying because one of these rednecks thought I wasn't dying quick enough and tried to take me out early. But he didn't finish it off, so I'm here.

I hear my mother moving around, and I keep my eyes closed, so she won't know I'm awake. I can't deal with any more crying right now.

But when I close my eyes, it's like I'm there again. This morning. The sun streaming through my windshield.

The baseball bat, the broken glass. The outline of some guy—the guy who attacked me.

And now I'm here, face aching, and the rest of me just numb. Numb.

Monday, 11:00 a.m., principal's office, Pinedale High School

CLINTON

"Where's Mr. Runnels?" *What the hell are cops doing here?*

"Come with us, son," the shorter cop says.

You know what I hate? When people think they can call you son or boy, just 'cause they're older than you. I'm not your son! I want to shout. I have a father! Still, I remember what Dad said about cops: "Always be respectful. A cool head and the word *sir* will get you out of many a situation, my boy. I know."

"Yes, sir." I follow them into Runnels's office. I start thinking maybe I ought to ask for my mother to be there. I mean, I didn't think there'd be cops. Are they supposed to question me without my mother there?

But I decide, nah. Why get her all involved? It's just a prank. But considering it involves the homo, she'd be trippin' if she knew. "Throw the book at him," she'd probably say. I'm still hoping to get this over quick.

So I follow the two cops into Runnels's office and sit down on another green plastic chair. One of the cops—the short guy who called me son—sits at Runnels's desk. The other one, a tall, skinny guy, sort of wanders around the room. The short one looks familiar. I wonder where I've seen him before. Then I remember. He was one of Dad's poker buddies back then. They used to come over our house Wednesday nights to play cards and drink beer. Couple times, Dad even let me sit with them and tried to teach me to play. Tried to teach me to cheat for him too. But I was too stupid to do it right. I was eight or nine. For years they did that. Mom hated it because they messed up the house. And this guy—they called him Junior—he and Dad had lots in common. I feel myself relaxing. It was the right thing, not calling Mom. Everything'll be fine.

But it's the tall cop talking now.

"I'm Officer Bauer, and this is Officer Reed. We want to ask a few questions. Okay? We'd appreciate your cooperation."

I nod. I don't say I'll answer them. "Yes, sir."

"You know a guy named Alejandro Crusan?"

"Sure. Alex. He's in my trig class. Government, too. I've got to sit by him because our names both begin with *C*."

Act casual.

Officer Bauer looks up when I say that. "You don't like sitting next to him?"

"Well . . . look, they say he's not a fag or nothing, though I'm not too sure. It's just, you never know what you could catch, being around someone like that.

16

I mean, what if he sneezes? Or bites someone?"

I figure now I'll get some big lecture about how I can't get sick sitting by him. Wouldn't be the first time. Instead, the tall cop looks back at Dad's friend.

Dad's friend—Officer Reed—says, "Well, sure. I can see how you'd think that. I mean, it's a real serious illness he has."

"Exactly. It's not that I don't feel for the guy, just—"

"You don't want to get sick."

"Right. Or my family to get sick either." I can tell Officer Reed is sort of seeing my point, so I keep going, trying to talk my way out of it. Lots of people agree with me. They're just too scared to say it. "I mean, why should we all have to be exposed to that? They told us before he came here that you couldn't get sick, just being near him. But I don't believe it for a minute. I mean, what if he cuts himself? He doesn't have those purple, blotchy things you always see on people with AIDS on TV. But still, there's all these molecules and particles and things, junk in the air. And what about dust mites?" I remember once, they told us in science class that dust is all people's skin and junk. *Excuse me*, but I don't want *that* guy's skin particles on me. "And did you hear about some people who say they got AIDS from a dentist? They said that couldn't happen either. I figure better safe than sorry." *Okay, stop now.*

I remember this time in grade school . . . well, I bite my pencils. And once this guy, Trevor Dornau, thought it would be funny to stick my pencils in his ears, so I'd be eating his earwax. What if Crusan thought it would be funny to spit on my pencils? Or even bleed on them? Could happen.

"Understandable," Officer Reed says. "So you must think it's a bad idea, them letting Alex go to school here?"

"Right. I mean, maybe if they'd put him in one of those plastic bubbles or something. I saw a movie like that once on TV—this kid went to school in a space suit. But they wouldn't have anything that high-tech in Pinedale. Or maybe he could take classes at home, on television or something. Don't they do that?"

Both cops are nodding.

"I mean, when you think about it, why's he have to go to school anyway? He's just going to . . ."

I stop. The cops aren't nodding anymore. I guess it *is* kind of cold to say he's just going to die.

"Anyway," I say. "That's what I think."

I look at the bulletin board behind Officer Reed's head and try to relax, so I think of Alyssa. I saw her yesterday after school, but from a distance. She had on my favorite shirt of hers, a pink one with these sort of thin sleeves you can see her arms through. Damn. I take a deep breath, and I can almost smell her. The perfume she wears is like the little white flowers on the bushes behind our house.

"And did you tell anyone else you felt this way?"

the tall cop, Bauer, asks.

I snap to. They know I did. That's why they're getting on me. "Sure. I had to tell Mrs. Gibson, my Government teacher. I tried to at least get moved to a different seat." Figures the two classes I have with Crusan are the only two where we sit in alphabetical order.

"Who else?"

"Mr. David, my trig teacher. Him, too."

"And what did they say?"

"Mrs. Gibson was real snotty about it." After I say that, I think I should have maybe put it different. But I remember how Old Lady Gibson looked at me, like people do when they think you're *stoooo-pid* and they've got to talk slow so you'll keep up. I hate when people look at me that way. "I mean, she said there was nothing to worry about. She blew me off. David was better."

"What did Mr. David say?" Bauer asks.

I don't want to get Mr. David in trouble, so I say, "He understood. He's got kids that go here. But he said he couldn't really do anything about it, and maybe my parents ought to talk to Runnels. I mean, Mr. Runnels."

What Mr. David said, actually, is that he would take that little Cuban out himself, if he could. *And* he moved my seat.

"And did they?"

"Did they what?" I'm still thinking about Mr. David.

"Did your parents talk to Mr. Runnels?"

"My mom, she took their side in the whole thing. She's like that. Liberal."

"What about your father?" Officer Bauer asks.

I look down. "He didn't say anything."

I look at Officer Reed, thinking maybe now's the time he'll say something about how he knew my dad. But Bauer says, "So what did you do then?"

The way he says it, I bet he already knows about the notes I left in Crusan's locker, telling him to get out of Pinedale. I did the notes on the computer. I didn't think they could trace them, but maybe they did, somehow. And yesterday, after Melody got back from spending the night there and was talking about how she was going to go back again next week, I got a little crazy. I rode my bike over there and chucked a rock through the window. I didn't think anyone saw me, but now I'm here, and I don't know what's up with the cops and everything. Are they going to make me pay for the window? Call my mother? I didn't think of any of that when I did it last night. I was just upset about Mel. I wanted him gone, and no one was doing anything about it. No one could do anything, even though most people I talked to agreed with me, people like Mr. David, who said, "It stinks that one person's rights interfere with everyone else's. But that's the way things are in this stinking country."

But I look at Officer Bauer and say, "I didn't do any-thing, sir. There was nothing I could do. I sat where I was told and tried not to breathe in too much. Ask anyone. Lucky, we only have those two classes together. I guess Crusan's in the smart class for English. I tried to stay away from him, best I could. But other than that, I didn't do a darn thing."

Monday, 11:00 a.m., special ed counselor Joyce Taub's office,
Pinedale High School

DARIA

Mondays,
I wait
by the side of the road
for
Alex Crusan's car.

Monday,
Mama says
I can go
if it
does not rain
and it did not
rain today.

I waited.
I like Alex Crusan's car.
The headlights
look like
big eyes staring.
I like Alex Crusan.
He smiles at me.

The big eyes were there.
I hid
by the side of the road
in leaves
that
crunched and
smelled
like rainy dogs.
Alex Crusan
can't see me
unless I
pop out.

I wanted to pop out.
I wanted to pop out
and say hello.
I wanted to surprise him.

The boy was there
in a blue letter jacket.
Wham!
Glass—smash!
Like ice
falling up.

Baseball bat,
blue letter jacket.
Alex Crusan
under the glass,
blue letter jacket.
Glass
like ice
falling up.
I could not run.
I ran.

I saw who did it.
I saw
the blue letter jacket.
I said it.

Monday, 11:15 a.m., Memorial Hospital

ALEX

I guess I must've dozed off for real because when I look up, Mom's gone. Which is better, really. Sometimes I can't take her crying on top of everything else.

But someone else is there. A candy striper in this dumb uniform that looks like it's from the 1950s, pushing a flower cart. I've seen her at school. Jennifer . . . Something, a little mousy, but pretty blonde, curly hair. I'm surprised she's here during school hours. She stands there, staring at me. I know what she's thinking. People who first see me think I'm going to look like Tom Hanks in that movie *Philadelphia,* where he lost, like, forty pounds and was covered in lesions from Kaposi's sarcoma. I don't look like that . . . yet. I can't think about the day I'll look like that. At least, I try not to.

I'm about to say something rude, like hasn't she ever seen anyone with HIV, working in a hospital.

Then I realize she's looking at my face. It's all bandaged, so I bet I look like a mummy. I go to touch it, but my hands are bandaged too. Nothing hurts. I must be doped up, which would explain why I'm sleeping so much. I feel tired right now, and I just woke up.

I say, "Jennifer, right?" It's hard to talk.

She's getting the flowers off the cart, and she practically throws the vase at me when I speak. But she recovers.

"Good save," I say. It's easier the second time.

She puts the flowers beside the others on the windowsill, then leans to get a roll of paper towels to clean the water she spilled. I get a pretty good view of her legs and . . . stuff. Good to know I'm not too doped up to notice that. Nice. Very nice. I have no illusions that a girl like that—or any girl—would be interested in me. But I'm still a guy.

When she stands, I repeat, "You're Jennifer, right?"

"Jennifer Atkinson." She doesn't come closer, which is no shocker. She folds two paper towels to make a thick square, then leans again to dab at the water. This time she leans forward, and I can see down the front of her uniform. "You scared me. I thought you were asleep."

She stands again.

"Sorry." I gesture at my bandaged face. "I'm Alex. We go to school together."

"I know who you are."

And, since she doesn't say it like go-away-and-please-stop-emitting-carbon-dioxide, I ask, "Who are the flowers from?"

"We're not supposed to snoop in the cards."

"It's not snooping if I ask, is it?"

She looks doubtful. "I guess not."

I back up. "If you don't want to talk to me, just put the cards on the nightstand."

So tired. Eyes . . . closing . . .

"No, that's okay." She steps sideways and stoops to wipe some more water. "They told us we can't get sick from casual contact." She looks at me, looking at her, and her face goes all red. "I mean . . ."

"You're right," I say quick. "That's totally right—you can't. Not many people around here seem to know that."

"My mom's a nurse. And I want to be a doctor. I got special permission to work here Mondays during school, and other days after. You can't be a doctor and get scared of sick people." She looks up and blushes redder. "I'm not saying this right."

She reaches out and fumbles for the cards. I want to tell her I'm not sick, not really, that maybe I'll never get really sick. But it's the first normal, human conversation I've had with anyone my own age since we moved to Pinedale, and I don't want to kill it by sounding like a public service announcement. So I say, "No, you're right. That's smart. But then, you must be smart if you plan to go to med school."

God, I sound like a moron. She ignores it and opens the first card. "From Mom, Dad, and Carolina." She pronounces Carolina's name right, unlike most people around here who pronounce it like the state. She opens the other card. "And this one's from Mrs. Adele Cole, Melody, and Clinton."

27

She looks a little surprised, and I almost laugh myself. Figures. Melody Cole is Carolina's best friend, but she's also Clinton Cole's sister. Weird that with all the things Cole and I don't have in common, we have sisters exactly the same age. Mrs. Cole is one of those moms who always acts like she's running for the title of World's Best Person. I figure she does it to make up for giving birth to an asshole like Clinton. So while everyone else is giving us the evil eye at Winn-Dixie, Mrs. Cole runs up to Mom in frozen foods to ask if we need help finding anything. She lets her daughter play with Carolina when pretty much no one else will. I know I should be grateful. But I wish I didn't have to be, you know?

"Well, I'm damn sure they aren't from Clinton," I say.

Jennifer looks at me funny, and I'm about to apologize for my language. Kids around here don't swear like they do in Miami and on the rest of the planet. It's possible she's shocked by the word *damn*.

But when I look at her, she's staring at the card.

She says, "I hope they throw that guy's ass in jail for what he did to you."

CLINTON

"I didn't do anything," I say again.

Okay, so I threw the rock. It wasn't a big rock, and I did it when no one was home. No one saw me. I knew from Melody that the Crusans go to Sunday night services at the Catholic church on Rolling Road. So that's when I went, last night around seven when the house was mostly dark. I parked my bike a block away, in front of that little retard girl's house. Then I hoofed it to the Crusans' place. It's a real fancy house with big trees and bushes, so I could sneak over under the leaves. I chucked the rock through the window and left. I didn't think it was a big deal since no one was there. But now the cops are here, so they must've found out somehow. And my ass is grass if my mom finds out.

They can't prove a darn thing.

"It would be understandable if you did something," Officer Reed says. "If you felt sort of . . . powerless."

"I was powerless. That's why I didn't do anything. There was nothing I could do."

"Are you telling me the truth, son?"

"Scout's honor." Though, of course, I'm not a scout

anymore. But I was one when I was eight. It was fun, till Dad said he couldn't handle any more of that camping junk. Now the whole thing of the cops being here, and not just Runnels, is starting to hit home, and my heart's thumping now, going *oh-shit, oh-shit, oh-shit* . . . till I think maybe they can see it through my shirt.

"Because there was an incident this morning."

Oh-shit. "This morning?" *Not last night?*

Officer Reed nods. "Someone attacked Alex Crusan's car. They hit it with a baseball bat."

"I don't know anything about that, sir."

And it's true. My lungs, they feel like helium balloons. It wasn't me. They don't know about the rock. They're looking for some other guy.

"I'd never vandalize a car, sir."

"I'm afraid there was more to it than that." I watch the tall cop's lips moving, stretching, then snapping back like in slow-mo. I realize he's talking like I already know what he's going to say. "Alex was driving the car at the time. He was badly cut by flying glass. They're treating this as a battery."

I stare at him, realizing. Battery. What does any of this have to do with me? I threw a rock, for God's sake. A stinking rock at an empty house. I didn't *batter* anyone. I wouldn't . . . I mean, I'd never actually hurt anyone. I look down at my hands, and they're shaking. They're trying to pin this on me. Jeez, they're trying to pin this on me.

Calm down, stupid. Stupid!

I try to think about what my dad would say to do. I know he'd say keep a cool head. Be respectful. I saw him talk his way out of a ticket once. That's exactly what he did. Smart, not stupid. I stick my hands between my knees to stop them shaking. I don't act guilty—he'd say that, too.

I say, "That's awful, sir. If I hear anyone talking about it, I'll be sure and let you know."

Officer Reed looks at the tall cop again. The tall cop looks at me.

"Son, let's cut the crap. There's a witness who identified you at the scene."

Monday, 11:30 a.m., courtyard, Pinedale High School

DARIA

First lunch,
me alone,
bench by the basketball hoop.
No one sits there,
just me.

I have baloney.
Mama uses brown bread.
Brown bread, not white,
orange cheese, not yellow.
The baloney smells good.
I put potato chips
between the slices.

The girls come,
one, two, three.
Don't sit.
They're not friends.
The yellow-hair girl's hair
shines like hair
in a commercial.

"Hear what happened?" she says.
"That guy
got his windows smashed."
Her voice sings up and down,
like Gramma's piano.

The others look.
"What guy?" they say.
I say, "Alex . . . Alex . . . Alex Crusan."
No one hears.

"That guy," she says.
"Hel-lo? You know.
The one from Miami, the one with AIDS."
"Alex," I say. "Alex."
No one hears.

"Who did it?"
"Don't know yet.
I saw his car
on the way to school.
The windshield was, like, totally smashed out."
"On purpose?"
"No doubt.
Bound to happen sooner or later."

"But who did it?"

I want to say
blue jacket.
I saw
the blue jacket.
I don't say it.
They don't hear.

"Who knows?"
The yellow-hair girl
sniffs the air.
My baloney.
She doesn't say it.

"Was he hurt?"
I want to know too.
She doesn't say.

She walks away.
The others go too.
Her hair is shiny.

Monday, 11:30 a.m., Memorial Hospital

ALEX

Jennifer left when the nurse showed up to change my bandages. I still haven't looked in the mirror. I feel less spacey, so whatever they gave me must be wearing off. I'm awake enough to notice I don't have a roommate. I wonder if that's because no one would want to room with me.

"He got it from a transfusion, you know," my mother says to the nurse as she follows her in.

"Mom . . ." I say.

My mother saw me talking to Jennifer when she came in, so now I can't pretend I'm asleep. She looks at me but speaks only to the nurse. Fine. She's mad. If I'd listened to her about not going out alone this morning, this wouldn't have happened. I give up on saying anything and submit to the whole *ER* routine. My mother hovers, getting in the nurse's way.

"Transfusion." The nurse looks at my face for the first time before dropping my bandages into a step-on garbage pail marked "Medical Waste." "That's very unusual nowadays. They run lots of tests on blood products now."

Darn near impossible, really.

"Poor child," the nurse says.

"Yes." My mother puts her hand on mine. "It has been a terrible misfortune."

The nurse takes out a needle and starts heading for the IV on my arm. I point to it. "What's that for?" I move my mother's hand over with the gesture.

"Just something for the pain," the nurse says.

"Is that why I'm so spacey?"

She nods. "Mmm-hmm . . . on this stuff, you should be feeling no pain."

"Don't give me any more."

My mother starts in. "Alex, I think you should let her."

"Please. I don't have to, do I?" I ask the nurse.

The nurse shrugs. "You want pain?"

"I'd rather have pain than be a waste case."

She nods. "I can ask your doctor."

"Yeah, do that," I say. "Thanks."

The second the nurse leaves, my mother starts in, first about how I'm feeling—fine. Fine.

Then she says, "Oh, Alex, I told you do not go this morning."

"I know. I'm sorry." There's no use arguing with her at this point. I just have to be sorry. So, so sorry. Sorry for wanting two minutes to myself without your whining. Sorry for being sick. Sorry for living. Sorry for not being sorry enough. My mother has protected me all my life—if she could have encased me in Styrofoam, she would've. She even held me back from starting kinder-garten until I was six so she could baby me longer. So, needless to say, she's barely holding it together with my having HIV. "Sorry," I repeat.

She touches my forehead. "The people in this place — animals. I told your father we cannot stay here, no matter what."

A week ago I'd have been dancing at this. But now I know it's my fault, that I'll be screwing things up for everyone like I'm always screwing things up for every-one. Even so, it *was* scary what happened this morning.

"We don't have to leave," I say. "It's just some nut job."

"Some nut job who attacks a seventeen-year-old boy with a baseball bat. No. I say to your father this is a bad place. He has to tell them transfer him back. Or else we go somewhere else. Another job."

"What about the health insurance?"

She sighs. "There's always Medicaid."

Medicaid. For poor people. She means if we lose our health insurance, and my illness makes us so poor we lose everything. Then Medicaid would pay for me. No way.

I change the subject. Again.

"Where's Carolina?"

"Home. I tell her stay in the family room. It has the least windows."

Windows.

Last night, when we were at mass, someone threw a

rock through Carolina's window. Then we had dinner and watched TV, so we didn't even notice until it was time to go to bed and Carolina stepped on glass in her bare feet. Who'd throw a rock through a little kid's window?

We called the police, but they weren't real helpful. *Que sorpresa*—what a surprise.

That was the first time anyone had done something like that. Other people have thrown stuff—bottles and junk—in our yard, but not the house. This felt different. It felt . . . personal. And now this, this morning. That felt about as personal as it gets.

Afterward we had a family meeting. Mom led it, of course. Dad sat and offered solidarity and fatherly wisdom. I know I shouldn't complain about my parents, that I'm lucky, really. Most people I've met with AIDS, their parents don't speak to them, much less hover and worry like mine. But sometimes, it's hard to feel lucky.

The upshot of our family caucus: The Crusan kids aren't supposed to leave the house unnecessarily, and never alone. I nodded along with the whole thing. It's not like I have any friends here anyway, and like I said, it *was* scary. That was until I realized I wouldn't get to spend time with my baby.

My baby is a three-year-old red Honda CR-V with a sunroof. Mom and Dad bought her for my seventeenth birthday. I know it was a stretch for them financially. Dad's always griping about what it costs to insure a seventeen-year-old driver, and I can't get an after-school job

("Would you like some fries with that, Mr. Cole?"). But my parents do that sometimes, indulge me because I'm sick. They don't say that's why, but it is. And hey, I'm seventeen. I want a car.

When I'm driving is the only time I feel halfway normal. One of my favorite things to do is, Mondays, I get up before everyone else and drive to Dunkin' Donuts, which is pretty much the only sign of civilization in Pinedale. I eat healthy the rest of the week—it's important to eat good foods and take about a million vitamins to help fight disease—but Mondays, I buy coffee for Mom and Dad and a dozen donuts. Mom and Dad love the vanilla bean coffee. The owner, Mr. Kahn, knows me. He always makes sure he has chocolate honey dip Monday mornings.

"I'm afraid that means no more Dunkin' Donuts," Mom said, like she knew exactly what I was thinking. She sighed. "Though I'll miss the vanilla bean."

I nodded. Carolina was screaming into someplace where only dogs could hear. She wasn't too happy about the new rules either. When I nodded, she glared at me like I was sucking up to my parents. I didn't bother saying anything because I knew I was going no matter what they said. One thing about having a limited life expectancy: it makes you more willing to take risks. I wasn't about to spend the time I had cooped up in this house in Pinedale, though I thought it was okay if Carolina did.

I figured once Mom smelled that vanilla bean, she'd get over it.

"I'm sorry," I say now. *Sorry. Sor-ry.*

"It isn't your fault, Alejandro. It is these . . . these people. They aren't human. They don't bleed as we do. They don't feel. As soon as you are out of the hospital, I will send you and Lina to live with Aunt Maria in Miami."

My mom's good at drama. She's still touching my arm. Sometimes I wonder if she touches me so much to prove she's not afraid to. Or that she doesn't hate me because of what's happened.

I move my arm an inch, trying to lose her, then feel bad and move it halfway back. "Why don't you go home and stay with Carolina?" I say.

"Why do you push us away, Alejandro?"

"I'm not pushing anything. But I know you're worried about Lina."

"Now, you think that. But this morning—you had to go out even though I tell you not to. You had to go. You complain about being lonely, having no friends. But we would always be with you if you let us."

I knew she wouldn't understand. I shouldn't say anything else. It'll start a fight.

But still I say, "When I'm alone, that's the only time I don't feel lonely."

She sighs. "*Que quieres decir, Alejandro?*" She touches my hair. "This is crazy talk."

"No, it's not. Because most of the time, when I'm with people, it's like I'm not there anyway. People treat me like I'm a science project or have the plague. Or they ignore me. You do it too."

She's looking at me like maybe it's the drugs. But my mind is clear. I'm just tired.

"Remember when I was eight, when Austin's dad took us fishing?"

"I remember Austin," she says, like she's glad I've said something that makes sense.

"He took me and Austin out. It was my first time fishing."

I lean back, remembering. The tubes and machines fade away. I'm on the ocean.

It was this perfect Miami day, the kind where the sky and ocean seem to meet so it's like you're inside a blue ball. You hate to turn the motor on and ruin it, so you just sit and let the fish come to you.

"I caught a fish that day," I tell Mom. "I remember Austin's dad helped me take it off. I watched the fish grunting while he removed the hook. 'What happens to it now?' I asked him. I didn't want to eat it.

"'We put it in a bucket with ice and water. It'll last a few minutes, maybe an hour. But, sooner or later, the air runs out, and then . . . fade to black.'"

"Alex," Mom says now. "What does this have to do with anything?"

"I'm like that fish, Mom. I'm flopping around in a

bucket of ice water, no future, nothing to hope for. I feel like I'm fading away."

"You have hope. You have a future. We must ask God for a cure."

"I've asked him. Forty million people with this disease have asked, and he doesn't listen. Or maybe he says no."

"No. God does not say no."

"He says no to babies in Africa. Do you know how many have died? He doesn't care."

My mother's hands go to her ears. "We just have to wait. You have been lucky so far."

"Yeah. Lucky. I won the damn Florida lottery." I remember the nurse, the gloves, the medical waste. "Why do you always have to tell people I got it from a transfusion?"

"Alex, we have been through this. If we tell people you got it that way, then they—"

"Don't think I deserve it."

"I did not say that."

"You didn't have to."

Can you believe that God will help find a cure, but still believe he gives it to people who deserve it? But I don't say it.

"It's no one's business how I got it," I say instead. "It shouldn't matter."

"It matters to some people."

"To you? Are you ashamed of me?"

She sighs. "I try to make it easier for you. This is not only hard for you, Alex, but for all of us—especially when people are cruel. I want to make them be kinder, to make them think."

For the third time in ten minutes, I say, "I'm sorry."

She puts her arms around me. "Oh, my poor boy. At least they caught the person who did this thing."

CLINTON

I didn't do it!

When they told me they thought I'd smashed Crusan's car with a baseball bat, I freaked. Polite and respectful went hurtling out the window. I started crying, yelling that I needed my father and I wasn't going to talk without him. They backed off then. They called Mom. It took her a while to get there, and they didn't let me eat lunch. I thought she'd be trippin' 'cause she had to miss work and come down there.

She was mad, all right. She was mad at the cops. She didn't take their side like I thought she would. She took mine. Actually, she was pretty cool about it.

"You have no right to question my son outside of my presence," she said (she talks like that). She said she was calling our lawyer (didn't know we had one) and maybe suing the school district (harsh!). She also told them I was home in bed when it happened this morning.

Which . . . uh . . . I wasn't. But she doesn't know that. She doesn't know anything. I'm keeping where I was my little secret. But I was, for sure, not waling on Crusan's car with a bat.

But that shut 'em right up. They backed off. One thing I'll say about my mom—when she thinks she's right, dammit, she makes sure you hear it.

They said it was all a big misunderstanding. I wasn't under arrest or anything. They were just questioning me. They couldn't do anything definite till they talked to Crusan. And he was in the hospital, too doped up to do any talking about anything for a while.

They let me go. They told her I shouldn't leave town for the next week or so. They'd be in touch.

Mom doesn't talk while we stop for lunch, or on the way home either. It's sort of weird, but I start thinking it's—maybe—'cause she believes me.

Boy, was I wrong.

First thing when we get in the house, she starts. "Oh, Clinton, I can't believe it. As if this family hasn't had enough problems."

I don't know if she means our family or Crusan's. So I just repeat, "I didn't do it."

But I can tell from the look on her face she doesn't believe me.

"Oh, my . . . I sent him flowers. I heard on the radio, and I sent flowers to the hospital. I had no idea my own son—"

"I didn't do it, Mom. Honest," I say. "You've got to believe me."

"This is my fault. I knew how you felt. You threatened to do something like this."

"No, I didn't. I never . . ."

I stop. The week before, when she said Melody could spend the night at the Crusans', I did say something. I said if she didn't stop letting Mel go over there, I'd have to do something about it, something desperate.

"Jeez, I didn't mean anything like that, like bashing a guy with a baseball bat, for Christ sakes. I don't do things like that. I'm not like that. Jeez, don't you know me at all? I just meant—"

I stop again. I don't know if I ought to tell her about the rock. Or the notes in Crusan's locker.

I decide to keep the info on a need-to-know basis.

"Meant what?" Mom demands.

"Nothing. I didn't do it. That's all. You've got to believe me."

She looks like she's going to say something else, but a key starts turning in the lock. Melody's home.

And she's crying.

"Carolina wasn't in school today. Mrs. Admire didn't want to tell us why, but before we left, she told me. It's 'cause her brother got hurt."

Mom gives me a look like shut up. I do.

My sister, Melody, is maybe my favorite person in the world. I feel for the kid, really. She's sort of young for her age, and she's a fat kid. I was the same way. That was before I started lifting, getting big enough to play football. Now I work out every day and look pretty good, thank you very much. But I still remember what it was like. I remember how people's idea of being nice was just not to bother you, *not* to call you names. When I was a kid, I used to go to school every day just hoping to be left alone. That's why I feel for Mel so much.

"I want to call Carolina," Melody says.

"She probably isn't home," I say. "Why don't I help you with your homework?"

"I know you hate her, Clinton." She gives a big sniff, the kind where you just know she hoovered up a ton of snot. Gross. "But she's my best friend."

Only friend, more like. The idea is a thing with teeth. In my mind I can almost see myself, hurling that rock. Not a great throw, but good enough to do what I planned. I picked the window 'cause it was on the side, behind the trees. But I could see that there was a canopy bed inside. So I'm pretty sure it was Carolina's room. *Jeez.* But I wasn't trying to do anything to *her*. They weren't home.

"I don't hate her," I say. "I figured if her brother's hurt, they're probably at the hospital, so she won't be home."

"Is he in the hospital?" Another sniff. "How do you know?"

Mom gives me another shut up look, and I shrug.

"I don't know. I'm going to do my homework. I can help you, maybe."

"Like you're so smart." My sister's in gifted and won't let anyone forget it.

"I think I can handle fourth-grade work," I say.

"You can call her after dinner," Mom chimes in.

Melody wipes her eyes with the back of her hand.

"A-all right," she says.

Mom sends her in to blow her nose. "And wash your hands too," she yells after her.

When the water starts running, Mom faces me.

"Now are you going to tell me where you were this morning?"

Jeez! She knows I was out.

"No. You just have to believe I wouldn't do what they're saying."

Monday, 2:30 p.m., bus home from school

DARIA

> *One time,*
> *I was on my bench at lunch,*
> *listening to my most favorite CD*
> *which is*
> *Pink.*
>
> *Kids say NO ONE*
> *listens to Pink*
> *anymore.*
> *But I do.*
> *I like her.*
>
> *I was dancing*
> *a little,*
> *to "I'm Coming Out,"*
> *and Alex Crusan*
> *was there.*

He said,
"You like Pink?"
"Yeah," I said,
"her hair."
"Me too,"
he said,
"she's not afraid
to be different."

Then he said,
"Would you ever
dye your hair
pink?"
And I laughed
and couldn't
even stop
laughing.

All the days
after,
he said hi
just hi
and I
liked him.

Mama worried that
I liked Alex Crusan.
She thinks
I am a baby.

She asked Mrs. Taub,
my counselor,
was it okay,
okay, me liking Alex Crusan?
I felt
stupid.

But Mrs. Taub said yes!

Mama said
I can like him
but not go
to his house.
"Don't bother him, Dari."

Mama would be mad.

But last night,
I went.
I didn't do anything,
anything wrong,
just looked
at his house
in the dark.

Then
I saw him.
Not Alex, the other boy,
the fat, mean boy.
He threw a rock.
I wanted to tell
but
I
didn't
tell
anyone
about
that
rock.

Monday, 2:30 p.m., Memorial Hospital

ALEX

Now that they stopped the medication, my head's clear. Unfortunately, that only helps me remember what happened this morning—in real time and surround sound.

Old Mr. Khan at the donut shop says he could set his watch by me. He opens at six Mondays, and that's when I get there. I have to go early to make it before school. Other mornings I work out with weights in the garage. Just because you're terminal doesn't mean you can't be buff. I'm getting better about mornings. When I was first diagnosed, I could barely get out of bed some days. Like, what's the point? That's what I thought. Now I make myself. But I still don't use a seat belt when I drive—what's the point when you're going to die anyway?

This morning I left the house around ten of, maybe even a couple minutes earlier because I was so worried about Mom coming down on me. I saw that girl, Daria, this Down Syndrome girl who lives on East Main, about a block from our house. She's always there Mondays when I go by. Maybe she's there other days too, or maybe she's waiting for me. I think she has a crush on me. I talk to her at school sometimes, just say hi, like whatever. No one else does, really. They let the disabled kids (*differently abled* they said in Miami, like the word made a difference, like it changed who they were) go to the regular schools—*mainstreaming*, they call it. It's supposed to make them fit in the real world. It seems like a bad idea to me if people are going to be mean to them. And they are. They're mean just like they are to me, call her retard or, at best, ignore her. I don't know if she notices—if she's smart enough to notice—but I think she does. First time I said hi to Daria, it was at lunch, and she was listening to music on her headphones, dancing in her seat. Everyone around was staring like she was from Mars, when she was only having a good time. So I walked up to her and said hey. Talked to her. And she looked like I was Ed McMahon with one of those big Publishers Clearinghouse checks. Since then I always say hi to her. I feel good seeing her smile.

None of which makes me a saint or anything, and I was probably worse before. But things look a lot different when you're seeing it from the other side.

Anyway, today Daria was out there, hiding in the trees like she does. It was barely light out, so I could just make her out in my rearview. While I was at the stoplight, I saw her. I was almost thinking about opening the window and asking her if she wanted me to bring her back a donut, just to be nice.

That was when I saw the guy.

He was on the other side of the car, in my right side mirror. He had on a Pinedale letter jacket. He was in the bushes, waiting too. I couldn't see him well.

What I noticed was the baseball bat. Now in Miami, you might carry a stick or something out walking in case a dog attacked you. But probably not a bat. And with the rednecks around here, dogs are practically like their children, so you definitely wouldn't, so it was weird.

But before I even had time to *process* that, I heard the crash. Like an explosion all around me. Then another. I looked up at the spiders covering the windshield. Then, it was like slow motion, something—glass—falling around me. It cut my cheek, then my hand, and I didn't know where to go, so I sat there. Frozen. Staring at the glass, the light, the colors, almost like it was pretty. Then I was down on the seat, trying to get out of the way. I could feel the wind in my face, hear the whiff of the bat, then more crashing all around me, and there was nowhere I could go.

The smashing stopped a second, and it dawned on me: I have my foot on the brake. I can drive. Even if I hit something, who cares?

I was still down on the floor, but I stomped the gas and drove away. I must've driven a quarter mile, not even seeing where I was. Then I managed to sit up, and I drove to Dunkin' Donuts. I was bleeding pretty bad, and I couldn't touch anything without getting hurt worse. Glass was everywhere, hanging from the broken window and on the steering wheel. But I stumbled up to the store and said, "Please," before I collapsed. I guess Mr. Khan called an ambulance. My mom said he called them, too, so he must have gone through my pockets and found my last name. I don't think anyone from school would have done as much for me.

The worst thing about this is, it's like the beginning of the end. Whether we stay here or move back to Miami, my parents are scared now. They're right to be, but now I'll be even more of a prisoner. They'll let me do less and less from now on.

I hear someone at the door, probably Mom, and pull my pillow over my face to pretend I'm sleeping again. I don't want to talk about moving or how crummy everything is. Or God. It only makes me feel worse.

But from my vantage point under the pillow, I can see it's not Mom. It's Jennifer.

Monday, 2:35 p.m., Cole residence

CLINTON

"Look, I said I didn't do it," I tell Mom again.

We're still in the front hall. I'm talking real soft so Melody doesn't hear us from the bathroom.

"You're making it very hard for me to believe that, Clinton. I know you weren't in bed this morning."

"But you do believe me about Alex. Don't you?" I hear begging in my voice.

Hers, too. "I want to. I want to believe that no son of mine would do something so cruel to a boy unfortunate enough to have this disease. I want to believe it, Clinton."

"Then believe me." I feel like screaming it. *Believe me!*

"I'm trying. There was a witness who says she saw you."

"What witness?" I didn't see anyone when I was out this morning.

"A girl. Daria something."

"I don't know any Daria." Then I remember and laugh. "She's a retard, a dummy."

"Please don't use those words, Clinton."

"But . . ." Then I decide not to argue. Why get her madder at me than she already is? "Sorry."

57

Mom sighs. "It would be easier for me if you'd tell me where you were this morning. Otherwise, I have to assume—"

"I can't," I say. Telling her where I was will make her feel bad.

She starts to say something else, but the phone rings and she goes to get it. I watch her, feeling like I'm up a creek and a gator ate my paddle.

Thing about my mother is, even though we don't always agree on things, she stands by me. Like today, with those cops. Or when I was little. Like I said, I was never long on friends as a kid—not like now. Once, in fourth grade, I got beat up by this kid, Tyler Grendi. My parents really got into it then. Mom wanted to call Tyler's parents and the school. Dad told her she was making me a mama's boy and what I really needed was karate lessons. They argued for hours. I guess both of them lost, 'cause Mom never called the school. I never got karate lessons either (though Dad did give me a talk about setting my feet when I threw a punch. He even let me hit him some and pretended it hurt). But at the end of the day, it was Mom who came to my room and said things would get better.

And it was Mom who got custody of us when they split up. Dad said the courts always give custody to the mother anyway. He didn't have money to fight her about it. But, thing is, he didn't even try.

I hear Mom in the kitchen, winding up her conversation.

She'll be back here any second, and I can't face her. It feels bad, having her think I could do something like that. Yeah, maybe I'm harsh on people, like Crusan or that Daria girl. But I'm only being honest. Isn't that supposed to be a good thing? That doesn't mean I'd hurt someone like that. Like, doesn't she know me any better? I want her on my side, like she always used to be. But I can't have that if I don't tell her where I was this morning. And I don't want her to know. I was at the Gas-n-Sip, calling Dad on the pay phone there. I didn't tell Mom because she's real mad at Dad about the child support thing. So it would sound like I was going behind her back, which I kind of was, or taking his side, which I was not. Best thing I can do, probably, is avoid her completely by helping Mel with her homework.

I hear the phone in the kitchen go click on the receiver thing, and I head for the stairs as fast as I can without running.

Melody's homework is pretty hard. She may only be in fourth grade, but she's in all these brainiac classes. It's social studies, which should be simple. I mean, you just flip to the questions at the end of the chapter, then flip back, looking for the answer in the reading. And it's not like I haven't learned about Benjamin Franklin five hundred times already. But today I can't look at anything long without getting all frustrated. Soon it's like she's showing me how to do 'em instead of the other way around.

"I guess I don't remember this easy junk as much as I thought," I say.

And I'm glad when she says, "It's okay. I'll do it myself."

But I'm less glad, a few minutes later, when she puts her pencil down completely and says, "Clinton, do you know what happened to Carolina's brother?"

I look at my trig book. I'm not sure what the assignment was, exactly, since I wasn't in class. But Mr. David usually assigns the page after the one we just did. So I figure I'll do that one.

"Clinton?"

"I think someone smashed his car window."

"But he's in the hospital. They had to do something else."

"Well . . ." I pretend I'm figuring a problem in my head. "I think he was in the car."

Melody looks at me, and her cheeks seem sort of pinker than usual, but she doesn't say anything. I go back to the math book.

After a minute Mel says, "Is Alex going to die?" in that honest, nosy way kids say things.

Eventually, I think. But when I look at her, she looks really scared, so I say, "I don't think so. Not from getting his window smashed."

The cops would've probably mentioned if Crusan was that bad.

"Carolina called last night. She told me someone

threw a rock through her window. She thought her parents might take her out of school." The phone rings again, and I hear Mom answer it. "Why would someone do that?"

I don't want to go there since that one *was* me. I look over at Melody's bookshelf, at her doll collection, because I can't look at the book anymore. I'm good at math. I tell myself that— *You're really good at math, doofus.* But if Melody's homework was hard to concentrate on, mine is impossible. "I don't know. I guess maybe they don't think her brother ought to go to school here 'cause he's sick. He could get other people sick."

"But that's not fair. Alex is nice. He lets us play with his computer games. And he can't help being sick. It's just 'cause he had a trans . . . trans . . ."

"Transfusion," I say, though I wonder if he really got it from a transfusion. Most people who have AIDS are homos, right? Crusan doesn't look like a homo, but sometimes you can't always tell. He talks like one sometimes with those big words he uses, acting like he's better than everyone.

"Right. What's a transfusion?"

"It's when you get in an accident or something, and you lose a lot of blood. So they give you some blood that someone donated." I remember last year, before the Crusans moved here, they had a blood drive for homecoming at school. A lot of people didn't want to donate 'cause they were afraid they'd get sick. You don't always know where those needles have been, no matter what they tell you. I was glad it was only seniors and alumni who could donate. Otherwise, I'm sure my friends would've been on me to give. And I'd have given . . . given *in,* that is. They aren't having a blood drive this year. I'm glad.

"Like when Dad and I were in that accident?"

She's talking about when Dad hit a tree last year, just before him and Mom broke up . . . which Mom said was *why* her and Dad broke up.

"You didn't need a transfusion," I say. "It wasn't that bad an accident."

"But if I had, would everyone be mad at me, like they're mad at Alex?"

"They're not mad at Alex."

"They're mean to him."

"They just don't want to get sick by being around him. That's different than being mad. It's a really bad disease he has. No one wants to take any chances."

"Carolina's around him all the time, and she's not sick."

That we know of.

"But it's a risk," I say. "People don't want to take the chance."

"If I got sick like Alex, would you still want to be around me?"

"Sure I would. I'm your brother."

"Then, why—"

"Look!" I'm yelling now. "I'm trying to do my homework. I don't have an IQ of one-fifty like you. I need to concentrate."

"Sorry."

We sit in silence a few minutes, but the numbers swim before me, and I can't do the problem.

Monday, 2:35 p.m., Bickell residence, out in front, near the trees

DARIA

> *I saw*
> *Clinton*
> *on a bike,*
> *riding by.*
>
> *I saw*
> *Clinton*
> *in a blue jacket,*
> *riding by.*
>
> *I saw*
> *Alex Crusan's*
> *red truck*
> *riding by.*

I saw
the baseball
bat
a blue
jacket
the crash-smash
glass.

I saw
darkness
no face
the blue
jacket
smashed glass.

I knew
who
it was.

I told them so.

Monday, 2:35 p.m., Memorial Hospital

ALEX

"More flowers?" I ask.

"You're awake." Jennifer examines my face, and I wonder for the first time how bad I'm going to look. Now that the painkillers have worn off, I'm conscious of the pain. I have a ton of stitches, and my face probably looks cut up and scary. I still haven't looked in the mirror. It's a game I'm playing at this point, to see how long I can *not* look. But I wonder if it will heal or if I'll have scars on top of everything. I can be like Freddy Krueger, that guy in the horror movies, with the burned-up face.

I don't want to look scary in front of Jennifer. I don't know why. It's not like girls have any interest in me. And it's not like she's a supermodel or anything, just an average girl with—sheesh—freckles on her nose. But I just—I don't know—like the idea of someone to talk to. She's the first girl I've met in Pinedale who's acted normal around me.

The first week at school, I was by my locker and this girl with long blonde hair walked by. Now I know her name was Kendall Barker, and she was way out of my league—especially now. But that day the planets aligned, and she was

66

(I'm pretty sure I'm not flattering myself here) checking me out. I'm not bad looking. I'm tall, tall and skinny, actually, but usually I can hide that by wearing baggy clothes. I always thought I had okay eyes. They're grayish. I started to say hi to her. Then some other girl whispers something, and Kendall looked at me like I was a leper and one of my fingers had fallen off and rolled down the hallway. That was the first sign I had that people here knew about me. The school isn't supposed to tell the students, but they did. I guess she was afraid I'd get her sick. But you can't get infected by talking to someone.

I could chalk it up to her being a bitch . . . but they can't *all* be bitches.

"You *are* awake, aren't you?" Jennifer says.

"What? Um, yeah. I'm awake. I was pretending to sleep in case you were my mother."

"That's kind of weird. I mean, your mom seems nice."

"She *is* nice. It's just . . ." I wave my hand in the air like, forget it, knowing I probably majorly screwed up her opinion of me. "What are you doing here?"

"I'm on break. Thought I'd come say hi. I could leave if you want."

"No!" I don't mean to raise my voice. Maybe I have a personality disorder in addition to HIV. "No, stay. My mother . . . I mean, it's frustrating. She's upset and it's my fault, and there's nothing I can do about it."

Shut up now, Alex.

Jennifer reaches up to touch her hair. Her blonde

curls are whipped into submission in a ponytail and two red barrettes that look like something for a younger girl, like Carolina.

"I guess I could see that." She takes out one of the barrettes and pushes the hair around. "Where is your mom now?"

"Home checking on my sister. Carolina wasn't answering the phone."

"Maybe she went to a neighbor's house."

"The neighbors haven't exactly been over with the Welcome Wagon."

"Sorry. That was stupid." She replaces the barrette. "Can you believe they make us wear this dumb hairstyle, to keep the hair off our faces? We're supposed to wear hats, too, but I pretend I lost mine. The nurses don't wear hats anymore, so why should I? Most places, the hospital aides just wear T-shirts instead of this dumb uniform. Pinedale is so retro—and not in a good way."

"I think your hair looks good like that." I think a hat might be kind of hot looking too, like nurses in those World War II movies, but I don't say it.

"Yeah, right." She takes out the other barrette. A piece of hair falls in her eyes and, on second look, she's a lot prettier than I thought. "Is Carolina your sister?"

"Right. I thought the school gave everyone a full briefing on my life history before I came here."

"They didn't . . . well, maybe a little. They had an assembly."

"I know. They aren't supposed to tell the students. That's the law."

"They didn't tell us everything. It was mostly about dealing with blood products." She replaces the second barrette.

"In case I started spontaneously bleeding at school or something?"

"I think it was more in case you got hurt." She gazes at my face, and I think with a twinge that I have, in fact, gotten hurt. That under the bandages are all the contaminated blood products everyone's so worried about. "They didn't do it to be mean."

"I know. No one does anything to be mean."

"Oh, I wouldn't go that far. I think some people are mean, just not everyone."

My parents wanted to sue the school for having that assembly, but I told them no. I told them I wouldn't go to school if they sued. Everyone knew already. It's not like they could make the school *un*-tell people by suing. I'm already the kid with HIV. If I sued, I'd be the kid with HIV who's suing everyone. I wish I could just be Alex.

"I used to play baseball," I say.

"What?"

"In Miami. I used to play baseball. I was a great hitter. I wanted to be the next Sammy Sosa. Do you know who that is?"

"The guy who was trying for the home run record a

while back, right? The guy who got in trouble for the corked bat."

"Right." I ignore the corked bat comment, which is still a sore point with me. "He got so screwed when you think of it. Roger Maris had that record—sixty-one homers—for thirty-seven years. Sosa got sixty-six that season. He's an excellent hitter. If he'd done it the season before, he'd have made the record books, at least for the year. Everyone would know about his record. He'd have been immortal." I stop, thinking about the word. *Immortal.* "But Mark McGuire had to come along the same season and do just a little better. Seventy runs."

"I remember," Jennifer says. "Chicago, right? I remember thinking that wasn't fair."

"Depends how you look at it. Sosa's great. McGuire's just better. Anyway, Sosa was my hero. I wanted to grow up and be like him, and like I said, I was a good player. And when I got diagnosed, the doctor said it was fine if I kept playing as long as I felt okay. Baseball's not a contact sport, so there was really no risk to anyone. And there's no reason to think I couldn't do anything I want."

"That's great."

"Yeah. Except people found out. Then a bunch of players quit the team. No explanation given. They found other players, but then a couple of teams forfeited games against us because they didn't have enough players show up. We were having a winning season, but we'd only played about half the games. I didn't want to ruin it for everyone else, so I quit."

"You copped out."

"Were you listening to the same story I just told?"

"Yeah. I'd have stayed on the team."

I laugh. "Yeah, right. You think you would have."

"No, really. I don't think anyone should keep you from doing what you want."

"Yeah. Everyone thinks they'd do something different. But after a while, you get tired of being a test case." I want to slap myself for the way I'm sounding. "Never mind. I wouldn't expect anyone to understand. You were nice to come visit. Tell me about you. Tell me about your plans for med school."

"That's really condescending."

"What is?"

"Being all sanctimonious—assuming I couldn't possibly understand. Actually, I think I *do* understand."

"You HIV-positive?"

"No. But while you were in Miami, ditching the baseball team, I was in Crystal Springs, getting drummed out of the ballet recital because everyone in town knew that my father was screwing his law partner."

"Ouch. What happened?" She looks pained, and I add, "If you don't mind my asking."

"No. Since it's you."

"Yeah, since it's me."

Which she ignores. "My father was a commissioner in the little town where I grew up. He planned to run for state senate. He and Mom were never, like, a perfect couple. But I thought they were okay, you know?" She walks to the door of the room, looks out, then comes back. "But about a week before Dad was going to announce his candidacy, there were these photos in the paper. Seems Dad's opponent heard about Dad's affair, so he hired an investigator with a long-lens camera. They got footage of Dad and Kimberley in his car."

"Doing what?"

Jennifer looks away. "What people do in cars."

I feel my face getting hot. She must see it too because she adds, "I mean, not that I've ever done that in a car. Or . . . I mean, anywhere . . . I just heard—"

"Sure."

"Anyway, the photo was on the front page of the local paper, with a black slash over the important parts. The bigger regional papers picked it up too. Dad was out of the senate race, him and Mom split up, and I had to go to school every day knowing everyone knew about it, until we moved away six months ago."

"And the dance recital?"

"My teacher said she thought it would be inappropriate for me to be in it. She refunded my costume deposit and everything. It was the first time I had a big part. Anyway, I guess she decided some girl from a *decent* family should do the Coffee dance from *The Nutcracker*."

"What a bitch."

She shrugs. "I sort of found out who my real friends were. And sometimes I'll meet someone from Crystal Springs who says, 'Is your father Harmon Atkinson?' and I have to say, yep. Yep, he is. And I vowed that I was never again going to let anyone force me out of something I wanted because of some problem of theirs. So I know what it's like . . . except the part about being sick, I mean."

"Yeah, there's that part."

She paces to the door again. "Okay, I'm sorry. I know you can't *die* from embarrassment . . . so maybe I don't really understand at all." She looks at her watch. "I ought to go. You're probably tired."

"No!" I want to get out of bed, disconnect everything, and kiss her for even trying to understand, but that would be too pathetic. "No. Don't go. I like talking to you. I'm so lon—I mean, they gave me a single room, and it's boring here."

She looks around, like she's seeing the room for the first time. "Yeah, I guess it would be. Didn't your mom get you any magazines or something?"

I shrug. "She must be too busy worrying." Which sounds lame, but why the hell *didn't* Mom get magazines? She's supposed to be so concerned, but she's not really thinking about what *I* need. Sometimes I think she acts that way because it focuses attention on her. She doesn't really care.

God, I am a shit.

"Oh, well. I'll bring you some tomorrow—we get *S.I.* I could have my mom bring them. She's a nurse. She works the early shift, so she could get here earlier."

"That'd be great." I want to ask whether she'll come in too, but I don't. I wonder if she has a boyfriend.

"I come after school. Or I could bring you books if you like books better?"

I nod. "Books are good. I like fantasy, magical worlds, stuff like that."

She smiles. One of her top teeth is a little sideways, and it just works on her. "Those are my favorites too. I just finished a good one by Garth Nix. I'll send it tomorrow." She looks at her watch again. "I really have to go, though. My break's been over for five minutes."

"Sorry."

"Don't be. I'll come back tomorrow, okay?"

She turns to leave.

"Jen . . . Jennifer?" I put out my hand to stop her, and I notice she backs away. When she realizes what she's done, she moves closer again, but not close enough to touch. She turns red, too.

Still I say, "My mom said they caught the guy who did this." I gesture at my face. "Who is it?"

She gives me a funny look. "I thought you knew. It was that football player, Clinton Cole."

Monday, 3:00 p.m., Cole residence

CLINTON

The doorbell rings. I jump. What if it's the cops?

It's not the cops. It's not the cops. *Calm down. Chill!* They said they had to talk to Crusan first. But he's in the hospital, all doped up. Probably Girl Scout cookies or something. I almost laugh at that. Who'd sell cookies at a time like this?

"Are you gonna go downstairs?" Melody asks.

"Nah. Mom will get it." I try and sound casual. Right.

But I'm not casual. I stare at my math book and chomp my pencil, which I have been trying really hard not to do anymore.

A minute later, there's footsteps on the stairs, then Mom's voice calling Melody.

I follow her down.

It's not the cops. It's Carolina Crusan. She looks tired and sad. When Melody sees Carolina, she runs and hugs her. I stay back.

"I missed you," Melody says. "I wanted to call, but they wouldn't let me."

She says *they* like my mom and I are involved in some

big conspiracy against her, and she's still hugging Carolina.

Carolina says, "My parents wouldn't either. Someone threw a stupid rock through my window, and now they're holding me prisoner. It's no fair."

"We're going to have to call your parents," Mom says. And the way she says it, I know she's dreading it.

"No!" Carolina starts crying. "They'll kill me. I wasn't supposed to leave the house. I wasn't supposed to ride my bike. I wasn't . . ." She keeps talking, but it's all lost in a flood of tears.

My mother stands, watching. Then she says, "Clinton, why not take the girls to the kitchen for a snack."

I don't want to. But on the other hand, I'm glad Mom's even speaking to me, so I figure I better do it. I gesture for them to follow me.

Once we get there, Carolina quiets down a little and they start arguing about what to have for snack. I wonder if they even told her about Alex yet.

"Can we make slice-and-bake cookies?" Melody demands.

"We don't have any." Even though I know we do. I just want to throw some Oreos at them and get it over with.

"Sure we do." Melody opens the door and takes out a roll of cookie dough. They're Halloween cookies with pumpkins in the dough. "See?"

I don't want to eat anything Carolina's had her hands in. But I figure they're just slice and bake. I decide it's probably okay. "Wash your hands first." I grab a handful of Oreos from the refrigerator before the door shuts. My mom keeps Oreos in the fridge since it's Florida and humid. My dad always said, "Never trust a woman who'd put cookies in the fridge. She'll be weird about other things too." I don't know, but it makes sense to me. I mean, who wants Oreos that got all gummy from the heat?

While they preheat the oven and cut the dough, Carolina gripes about her parents. "They only care about Alex. They're so mean. Everything's about Alex, Alex, Alex. He's like a prince, and he ruins everything. And if I say that, I'm bad for thinking it."

"My brother's the same way," Melody says.

"Um, am I in the room?" I joke, though I don't feel much like laughing. I'm thinking about what Carolina said about her brother. I go to open the oven door, and I catch my reflection. Funny how, when you see your face by accident, it looks different than when you look on purpose. I seem like I'm ten pounds heavier than I thought—my chin is like a turkey's. I peel one of the raw cookie dough pieces off the sheet and shove it in my mouth.

"Pig," Melody says.

"Yeah, like you'd never do that," I whisper. "Fat slob."

Melody glances over at Carolina but doesn't say anything. I say, "I didn't mean that."

She sort of nods. But that doesn't stop her looking like she's about to cry.

I am a big, fat jerk.

After they put the cookie dough in the oven, the girls sit down.

"My mother's gonna kill me," Carolina says again. "She'll freak. She was calling me before, telling me lock the doors and stay in rooms with no windows."

Windows.

"Because of the rock?" Melody says.

"Yeah. I stepped on some broken glass and hurt my foot."

I notice for the first time she has a bandage on her foot under her sandal. I wonder how bad she got cut. Like, did she get stitches? God, I just wanted to scare them. I didn't want to hurt a little girl. Maybe Mom's right not to trust me. Maybe I really *am* a bad person.

But I can't stop wondering if she could bleed on our kitchen floor.

"I was so scared to stay in the house by myself," she's saying. "Mom's with my brother, and Dad's at work. I mean, what if someone came to the house and did something?"

"I don't think they'd do that," I say.

"They threw the rock. They do all sorts of stuff to Alex. My mother calls them animals, and if they're bad enough to do those things, maybe they'd do other stuff too."

"I'm sure they . . ." I stop. I was about to say I'm sure they aren't that bad, but I can't get the words out. *Is* throwing a rock as bad as smashing someone's windshield? I don't think so, but Carolina cut her foot. I did that to her. That's something. "You'll be fine," I say finally.

The oven timer goes off at the same time the doorbell rings.

"Oh, no." Carolina starts to cry again.

It's Mrs. Crusan. Even though she's sort of a dark-skinned Cuban, her face looks white. She rushes toward Carolina.

"Oh, Lina, I was so worried. How could you do this?"

"I was scared at the house. Please let me stay here, Mommy. Just today."

"No." Mrs. Crusan gives me a look like I'm a serial killer or something. "No. You cannot stay here. You cannot come here ever again."

Monday, 3:00 p.m., Bickell residence

DARIA

Policeman
here
in our kitchen.
Scary.
Mama is
mad.

"I don't like
what you're implying."

"I'm not implying
anything, ma'am."

"My daughter
has no reason
to lie."

"It's not a matter of lying,
ma'am.
Just if she might be
mistaken somehow."

"She's not,"
Mama says,
standing up.

"Any witness can
make a mistake.
It's not just because she's — "

"She didn't
make a mistake."

"The boy's mother says
he was home."

Mama
looks mad,
looks at me.
"Did you see him,
Dari?
Did you see?"

I don't know
what
to
say.
How to say.

"*Daria, listen,*"
Mama says.
"*Listen.*"

"*Bike,*"
I say.

"*What?*"
the policeman
says.

"*On a bike,*"
I say.

"*On a bike?*
Clinton Cole?"
I nod.

"*Green one,*"
I say.

"*We can check*
that out."
He leans down.
"*Did Clinton Cole have*
a baseball bat?"

I don't know.

"Dari,"
Mama says.
"It's important.
Did the boy
have a bat?"

I saw
Clinton
on a bike,
green bike.
I saw a baseball bat
smash
Alex Crusan's
car.

I don't know.

"Daria?"

"Dari?"

"Did you see Clinton Cole?"

"*Threwarock.*
Broke
brokeawindow."

"*What?*"
the policeman
says.

Mama sighs.
"*Not a rock.*
A baseball
bat."

Slow down,
Mama always says,
Slow. Down.

"*Threw*
a
rock,"
I say.
"*House.*"

Mama says,
"*I'm sorry,*
Officer.
She seemed so sure."

"No."
The policeman
nods.
"No, she's right."
He looks at me.
"Someone threw a rock
through the Crusans' window last night?"

Mama looks.
"Daria,
were you at Alex Crusan's house
last night?"

She will
be
mad.

I nod.

The policeman says,
"Did Clinton Cole
throw a rock
through
the window?"

I nod
yes.
"Girl's
room."

Monday, 3:45 p.m., Memorial Hospital

ALEX

Just what I wanted: parents in surround sound.

"He must listen to reason," my mother says.

"Let the boy think, Rosario." That's my father.

"But he didn't do it," I say to the phone.

My mother is home now. Turns out my sister, Carolina, pulled some stupid stunt, running away to her friend, Melody's house (which also happens to be Clinton Cole's house). Mom had three heart attacks and is out for blood. Now Carolina's home with Mom, and Dad's here live and in person with me.

But that doesn't stop Mom from invading my ears.

"There was a witness, Alejandro. She saw him."

"I saw the guy who broke my windshield. It wasn't Clinton."

"Who was it then? Who?"

"I . . . I don't know."

I gesture at Dad like, *Help me, puh-leeeeze.* He shrugs and mouths, *What is she saying?* I hold the phone away from my ear so we can both hear her loud and clear.

"A boy in a letter jacket, though. You say a football

player. It was dark, Alex. Maybe you don't see so well. It was such a terrible thing. Maybe . . ."

She keeps going, but I've stopped listening.

"She is very upset, Alex," Dad says.

No kidding? I mouth.

"What?" Mom says. "What did he say?"

"Nothing," I say into the phone. "Look, I know it wasn't Clinton. Clinton's . . . *mas gordo.*" I can see the guy with the bat's outline, tall and slim.

Mom's voice starts again, like a scratched CD that plays over. "Do not do this, Alex. Do not let being afraid keep you from saying what is right."

Jennifer said something like that, about me quitting the baseball team. I wonder if she's gone for the evening, or if she'll come back to say good-bye. It's almost eight. She probably left. She probably does have a boyfriend— maybe some big, dumb football player who needs her to do his homework for him, so she rushes home.

Doesn't matter.

"I'm not scared, Mom. But I know it wasn't Clinton. If it was him, I'd say it—I can't stand the guy."

But I wonder if maybe I'm wrong. Maybe I don't want it to be Clinton because that would mean there's someone I know, someone I sit next to in class, who hates me enough to want me hurt bad. Is that possible? Somehow it's easier to think it's a stranger.

"No," I say aloud. "No, that isn't it."

"This boy does other things," Mom continues. I look

at Dad, and he shrugs. "The police just called. They say there is a witness who saw him throw the rock in Carolina's window."

"Who is the witness?"

"A girl—Daria someone."

"Daria Bickell? She lives around the corner. But she's not . . . maybe she just made a mistake."

I can picture Mom at home, pacing, talking with her hands. "She has eyes, Alejandro. And she knew about the rock. The police didn't tell anyone about it. She knew. She told them about it all on her own."

So Clinton threw the rock. I believe *that*. Probably he's one of the people who left notes in my locker, too.

I want to kill him for hurting Carolina. For hurting my family. Even if Clinton didn't attack me this morning, maybe he would have, given the chance.

They'll probably never catch the guy who did this to me. But if they think it's Clinton, they'd put Clinton in jail awhile. If they only tag Clinton for the rock, they'd probably let him off. He shouldn't get off that easy. He hurt my sister. He made us all scared to leave the house.

So I say, "I don't know. Maybe."

"He is a bad boy, Alex. I was so afraid that Lina was at that house."

And I know that's true. They're all afraid, even Dad, who's usually calm and normal. When Mom called him about Carolina, he took off work to come here. He can't do that all the time. I hate that they have to be afraid, and

I hate being responsible for it. Maybe they'd be less scared if they thought they'd caught the guy. It would be worth sacrificing a scum like Clinton Cole for that. And what do I get by coming clean? I piss off my family for what—for Clinton Cole? Will telling the truth change anything? Will Clinton stop being like he is? No, and no. He'll go "suckerrrr" and move on with his life. That's what he'll do.

"I'll think about it," I say to Mom.

That's when the nurse comes in, saving me. "I have to look at those stitches."

"Look, Mom," I say to the phone. "The nurse is here. I have to go."

"Okay," she says. "Fine. Go."

I hang up and look at Dad. He's been quiet most of the time, but it's good. Someone in this family should be quiet. The nurse pulls on her rubber gloves to start checking my stitches.

Dad puts his hand on my shoulder.

"You should do what you think is right, son."

Monday, 10:00 p.m., Clinton's room

CLINTON

"You crossed a line, Cole."

It's my friend Mo on the phone. I look around my room, like the right thing to say is written someplace there.

Mo keeps going. "I mean, none of us wanted him in school with us, but taking a baseball bat to the guy — what if you'd killed him?"

"I didn't attack him."

"Yeah, whatever."

He's gone before I can explain.

That's pretty much how it's been since Carolina and her mother left. I sprayed the kitchen with Lysol, and Melody hollered at me. The phone's been ringing so much you start feeling like that's just the normal sound the world makes. Mom stopped answering it. I only did this time 'cause I saw Mo's name on the caller ID and hoped he'd be a pal. My other so-called friends haven't called. It's okay to talk big and tough, but now they're all righteous, like I'm scum and they're Mother Stinkin' Teresa. Hypocrites!

Melody's in her room, crying. No one's talking to me.

I wish I could talk to my dad. I sure miss him sometimes.

Mom can't understand why I even want to talk to him. She thinks he's pretty worthless on account of his drinking and the money and all. I guess I'd think that too, if I was her. But he's my dad. If I think that, then what have I got left?

Besides, there's something I always remember times when I start getting mad at him. It's about my name.

My father was the one who named me Clinton. My mother wanted to name me after her grandfather, whose name was Willard, so I'll always be grateful she didn't get her way. But Dad insisted on naming me Clinton after Clint Black, the singer. He says he got Clinton because of this song he heard on the radio, "Killin' Time."

It's about this guy who realizes his drinking's a problem, and it'll probably end up killing him, but he can't help himself. The summer I was born, my dad says he got a tape of that album and listened to it all the time.

Another song that was on the tape was called "A Better Man." "If you let me name him Clinton," he told my mom, "it'll be a sort of reminder that that's what I'm trying to be. A better man." And Mom gave in and let him.

So when I get mad at him, that's always what I remember, that he was trying to be better for me, even if he didn't get it completely right.

Monday morning's when I call him. Every Monday. Dad has trouble getting out of bed after the weekend. At work they told him if he misses another day, he's gone.

So I promised I'd call and wake him, Mondays. Sometimes he even talks to me, tells me what's going on in his life. Usually he doesn't have time. I use the Gas-n-Sip pay phone so Mom won't get the bill and get all mad. Or, worse, think I'm pathetic for calling him when he never calls me.

Today I was out the door at ten till six, on my bike. It was cold out this morning, even though it's only October. I passed that retard's house on East Main. She was outside. I know she's telling everyone she saw me, and I guess she did *see* me. But she didn't see me wale on Crusan, 'cause I didn't do that. I didn't even *see* Crusan. I'd have noticed him. There aren't many people out that time of day, and Crusan drives that sweet, red Honda SUV—typical rich Cuban car. Meanwhile, I'm still sweating on two wheels. Dad promised me a car for my sixteenth birthday. But what with losing his job, I never ended up getting it. He said it was okay 'cause biking was better for me. "Keeps the weight down" was what he said, though I tried not to hear him.

When he picked up the phone this morning, I could almost smell the Jack on his breath. "Leave me alone," he growled. I called back, but he didn't answer. Don't know if he made it to work. I'm trying not to care, either.

I think about calling Mo back. But what would be the point? Mo and, I guess, *all* my so-called friends think I'm scum. Just like that—on the word of a retard. I wonder if all the guys on the team hate me too.

It isn't fair. Everyone was with me. They all wanted Crusan out as much as I did. Mo laughed when I called Crusan out that day in the cafeteria. Now they're all suspecting me. Ragging on someone is *not* the same as beating them with a baseball bat. What happened to innocent till proven guilty?

I turn out the light. Mom's downstairs. Mel's still bawling, and I think she's pouring it on just to make a point. I pull my pillow over my head to block it out, but I can't block out my thinking. Like, what if I'm wrong? What if I really am a bad person, and that's why everyone can believe this so easily? I mean, I chucked a rock through a little kid's window. What would it be like if that happened to my sister? What would I do to the guy that did it?

I'd kill him.

I get up, put on my shorts, and head to Mel's room. At least there's one person I can clear the air with.

She's at her desk, trying to study. The only light on's the desk lamp, and she's squinting. I try and remember if I studied much in grade school. Don't think so.

But Melody's studying. Or at least she's staring at her math book. When I get closer, I see her hands are covering the pages. I turn on the dresser lamp. It's shaped like a cat, and its stomach glows.

"You okay?" I say.

"No." She looks up. She's not crying anymore, at least. "I mean, yes. I mean . . . Carolina was my best friend, Clint. If she leaves or something, I won't have anyone to play with."

"That's not true."

"It is. Even she only hangs around because she can't make other friends 'cause of her brother."

That stabs at me. I figured it was probably like that, but I sure as heck didn't want Melody to know. I plunk down on her bed.

"Did she say that?" I ask.

"Of course not. She didn't have to. Look at me." She gestures at her body. "Before Carolina, I didn't have *any* friends."

"You talk about people at school—Taylor, and Alexa."

"Yeah, at school. Sometimes people let me sit by them at school 'cause I'm smart. But Taylor had a pool party and invited half the class and not me. The only one who asks me to her house is Carolina, and it's because no one likes her, either. For real, Clint. You can't look like me and have real friends. You know that."

It's no use arguing. I know it's true, and so does Mel. I say, "I bet she likes you now, once she got to know you. You're the best."

And even that, I know, might be a lie.

"I can't wait to grow up," Mel says. "I'm going to be a famous writer. Then everyone will want to be friends with me."

I remember thinking that kind of thing too. Not

about being a writer, but that I'd grow up and show them. And I have, being on the football team, popular. I am really one of the most important people at school now. At least till today. Now I'm as big an outcast as Crusan, and I didn't even do anything major.

"It'll be all right," I say.

"Sure."

When I go back to my room a few minutes later, I'm still thinking about that, about being miserable and wanting to grow up so things will be better.

I wonder if Crusan thinks that way ever. But in his case, it's not likely to happen. I wonder what that would be like—*knowing* you're not going to grow up.

Monday, 10:00 p.m., Daria's room

DARIA

> *Mama isn't*
> *mad now.*
> *She says good night.*
>
> *Mama is*
> *happy.*
> *Thinks I did*
> *a good thing.*
>
> *"Daria?"*
> *She stops*
> *at the door.*
>
> *"Yeah, Mama?"*
> *My head*
> *squooshes*
> *the cold*
> *soft*
> *pillow.*

*"Are you sure,
Daria?"*

*"Yeah, Mama.
Sure."*

ALEX

Night is when I think about dying. That's what I'm doing now, after midnight in the quiet hospital.

When I was first diagnosed, Mom and Dad thought it was really important for me to get my sleep. They said lights out at nine-thirty. So I'd lie in bed, thinking. During the day, you worry about school, math homework, all the normal, everyday stuff. But at night, when it's quiet, that's when all the thoughts you didn't have during the day, the thoughts you didn't *let* yourself have, swim up to the surface and float there so you can't sleep.

"Pray," Mom told me. Her answer to everything. I tried, but it didn't help. Sometimes, I could lull myself to sleep by repeating the Lord's Prayer over and over, but I didn't think that was what she meant.

So I tried logic. "I feel fine," my logical self said to me. "I could live to be a hundred," Logical Me said. Logical Me knew all the details about my disease, all the stuff I'd studied like it was a textbook for school. All about incubation periods and aggressive treatment and people who've been around for years. "You're fine," Logical Me repeated. *Finefinefine . . .*

"Who are you kidding?" I told him. "No one else you know has to deal with this. Your T-cell count could drop to a hundred tomorrow, and you'd be gone."

Logical Me didn't have an answer for that.

The sucky thing about being sick is not being able to talk about how scared I am. I don't want to worry my parents any more than they already are, so I stay quiet. Or lie about what I'm thinking, feeling. But you can lie to everyone but yourself, and that's why I can't sleep nights.

So finally what I started doing was, I didn't sleep. I mean, I slept, but I'd stay up watching television or playing on the computer until I was so tired my eyes started shutting and I couldn't help but sleep the second I hit the pillow.

I like it better that way. I don't like to think about that time when my body won't move anymore, and I'll just be a thing in a box. And then I'll be nothing at all. No one else I know thinks about that as their future. And I never do during the day, either. But after midnight, when there are no noises anywhere, there isn't much else to think about.

So I'm lying here, thinking. My body feels stiff. My fingers feel like someone poured plaster through them, like they can't move. The hospital brings the feeling closer.

Forget it. I find the remote and turn to Nick at Nite. It's a *Cosby Show* rerun, where the kids find a lost puppy, and Dad lets them keep it.

I know them all.

Tuesday morning, various locations, Pinedale High School

CLINTON

"Hey, Andy. Could I copy yesterday's assignment off you? I missed class."

Andy looks down.

"Um, I don't have it with me. Maybe ask Mrs. Gibson."

"Sure." I try and smile, even though I know Andy always has the assignments. I copy notes from him when I cut, and sometimes even when I just didn't pay attention in class.

"Sorry, Clint," Andy says. He turns away.

I sit. The desk by mine—Crusan's desk—is empty. Everyone who comes in looks at his desk, then at me.

Soon my face hurts from smiling.

The same thing happens second period, and third. Even people who were completely on my side about not wanting him in school with us avoid me now.

Fourth period, Alyssa Black, who should have been my homecoming date by now, passes me a note. I unfold it like a starving cat on an anchovy pizza. I can practically feel what it would be like, having her fingers touching me.

I read it:

Sorry I didn't say hi Mom says I can't talk to u CU around.

A

I crush the note in my fist. My heart feels like there's a bowling ball wedged up inside it.

At lunch I sit in my regular spot outside by the basketball courts. I'm one of the first there. I watch my friends, Andy and Brett and Mo, come in and get their lunch trays, then sit nearby, but a few feet down so I have to decide whether to move closer or sit there like an idiot. I remember that from my fat days in grade school.

I still don't like books much. But now I wish I had one, like those brainiac kids who sit in the cafeteria reading. I always thought that was just sad. But now I wonder if maybe they're reading to keep from doing nothing.

My friends finish their lunches in record time and stand. As they pass, they look at me, but like they're trying not to look, you know?

"See you at football practice," I say.

"Will you be there?" Brett blurts, then adds, "I mean, I wasn't sure if you'd be there."

"Sure, I will be." But I'm thinking, *Oh, God. Will they kick me off the team over this?* Being a football player was pretty much the best thing that ever happened to me. It's my life. Losing that would be worse than jail, worse than anything.

They walk away, saying, "See you there," except Mo, who says nothing.

I watch them, and I get that old sinking feeling I used to get when I had no friends and used to sit alone all the time. But that's not the way it's supposed to be. I've got friends. I hang out in a pack with a bunch of guys, and they're not just school friends, either. Practically every weekend, I've got something going.

Like, this one time, couple months before Mom threw Dad out, we all drove over to Leesburg—Andy, Brett, Mo, and I. Mo had just gotten his new ride, and since there's nothing much to do around here, we decided to head over to Leesburg.

Problem was, there's nothing much to do in Leesburg, neither. I mean, once you get done eating at the Pizza Hut.

"What's next?" Brett said. "Cow tipping?"

"No thank you, sir." Mo laughed. "Those cows can get *mean*."

So we were driving up and down the road, saying how dumb it was to go there, when suddenly Andy points to a Wal-Mart at the next intersection.

"My cousin's from Leesburg. He says that's where everyone hangs out on Saturdays."

"Wal-Mart?" To me, that sounded even sadder than what we do in Pinedale, which is either hanging out at people's houses or the parking lot of the Gas-n-Sip.

"Like, *girls* will be there," Andy said.

"At *Wal-Mart*?" I was still saying. But everyone else was down with going there, and a minute later we were pulling into the parking lot.

No one much was inside, a bunch of moms with little kids and some guys at the snack bar who looked about as bored as we felt. For sure, no girls. After about ten minutes, looking at steering wheel covers in the automotive section, Mo said, "This is lame. Let's cut bait."

"No, wait," Andy said. "I got an idea."

Then, he tells us about some cousin of his ("a *different* cousin") who's a real joker. "He went to housewares and set all the alarm clocks to go off, like, one minute apart."

"What's the point of that?" I said.

But Mo was grinning. "Don't you get it?" he said to me. "You set 'em for, like, *closing* time, then someone has to go turn 'em all off before they can go home."

I still thought it was a pretty dumb idea. But the other guys were acting like it was hilarious, so I went along. I didn't want them thinking I was too stupid to get the joke. Really, I sort of wanted to get home. Mom was away at some judges' convention with the guy she works for, and I wasn't sure if Dad was with Melody, or if she was sitting home alone, watching too much TV and eating too many Oreos. But I figured I'd do it and get it over with.

There must've been thirty alarm clocks, from the big superhero kind to the smallest travel alarm. When we set the last one, I said, "Okay, all done. We can go now, right?"

"No, dumbass," Brett said.

"Who you calling dumbass?" I said, sort of edging closer. Brett was not one bit smarter than me.

"You, dumbass. We have to stick around so we can watch for when they go off."

"But it's like"—I looked at my watch—"almost an hour till closing."

"Chill, Clint," Mo said. "You got anything better to do?"

I didn't say anything. I couldn't tell them about Dad or Mel or the Oreos. I kept my mouth shut and tried to think about how funny it would be when all those clocks started screaming.

When the first alarm went off, I started giggling. Mo nudged me to shut up. But really, you could barely hear it over the Wal-Mart noise.

The second wasn't much more. But a minute later, they were all ringing and this Wal-Mart employee, a geeky guy in a cheesy-looking uniform, comes over and starts turning them off. He's trying to put them back on the shelves, too. I forgot all about Dad and Mel and wanting to go home 'cause I was about busting a gut, laughing, and so was everyone else.

The guy didn't really notice at first because of all the clock noise. But then he turned and saw us.

"You!" he screamed. "You four!"

They were still ringing. But the guy didn't seem to care anymore 'cause he was running toward us, long, nerdy arms flapping. We all got up and ran to the front of the store. The guy's yelling, "Stop them! Security! Stop them!" and these two big guys try to block the door, but my friends all got out.

The only one they caught was me.

They tackled me. I was yelling, but they dragged me to some kind of store security office. The nerdy guy wanted to call the police, but once the security guys found out what they were chasing me for, they decided to just call my parents. Luckily Dad still had his cell phone back then. After they told him the problem, I asked if I could talk to him.

"What the hell's this about, Clinton?" he said.

But he sounded sober, so I said, "Will you please get Mel from the house before you come here? Please."

When he and Mel got there, he acted like it was all some big joke, saying, "Boys will be boys." Even when the manager got all huffy and told him I was banned from Wal-Mart for life, Dad just laughed and said, "We'll just shop at Target then." And when we got out to the car, he looked at me and Mel real serious and said, "This is just going to be our little secret, okay? No reason at all your mama needs to know about this—no reason at all." That was the thing about my dad. He'd take your side in things. And even when we went to Wal-Mart a few months later for back to school, and I had to wear my baseball cap so the manager wouldn't recognize me, I never told her.

That Monday, when I saw my friends at lunch, I got on them for leaving without me. Brett was joking, "Hey, survival of the fittest. You gotta leave behind the weak members of the herd."

But Mo said, "Nah, that ain't true. You took a fall for us, Clint buddy. We won't forget."

I felt real good when Mo said that, like I'd always have good friends. But now, I know Brett was the one telling the truth. I don't have any.

My so-called friends are still standing ten feet away. Not one of them looks at me.

I think maybe I'll go to the library.

Isn't that just sad?

Across the sidewalk, I notice that retard girl who accused me. I've seen her sitting by herself other days. But today Kendall Barker and some of the cheerleaders are around her, acting like she's their little pet or something.

"He'll be okay."

I look up, surprised. It's the first time anyone's talked to me on purpose all morning.

"What?"

"Alex. I saw him at the hospital."

I don't know the girl's name—Jennifer something, who's president of National Honor Society. She never talked to me before, and I never cared. Now she looks at me like I'm a fly on a pile of dog crap.

"I thought you should know you haven't gotten rid of him. He'll be back in school soon, no thanks to you. He's not going to die."

I gape at her. "I didn't touch him."

"Save it." She starts to walk away.

I sit there a second, shocked and mad sort of duking it out for my feelings.

Mad wins. "Hey!" I yell after her. "What have you got to do with it?"

She stops. "I'm a friend of Alex's."

"Sure you are." When she keeps standing there, not answering, I ask, "Ever been to his house?"

"No. We're friends from school."

"How 'bout his car?" I say. "Ever eat lunch with him?" I know she hasn't. I've seen Crusan sitting alone enough times. He's got no friends at all, not even fake friends like mine. "Do you choose him for your lab partner in science class?"

"Alex and I don't have science together."

"How about the others? He's in those smart classes. You must have something with him. You ever do a project with him? You ever sit by him, even?"

She starts to turn again. "I don't have to answer that. I'm not the one who—"

"'Cause the answer's no, right?" I'm standing now, walking toward her. "Right?"

"Shut up, you . . . you get away from me."

"It's no." I'm practically singing it. "No. You're no better than me. You like to think you are. But you're as afraid of catching something as anyone."

"Shut up!"

"Or maybe you don't want your friends seeing you with him."

"Screw you." I can see the anger in her eyes. It looks like it could come out and zap me, almost. I don't care. I hate her.

"Know what I can't stand?" I say. "People who think they're up there . . ." I point at the trees. "When really, you're as down here as me and everyone else."

"I don't have to talk to you."

She turns and walks away.

"No, you don't *want* to talk to me. And it's 'cause you know I'm right."

She's practically running now. People are staring, and I laugh. I laugh.

But then it hits me. If Crusan died, would they be accusing me of murder?

I stop laughing quick.

Fifth period, the kid from the office hands me a note from Mom. Skip football practice, it says. We're going to see a lawyer.

Tuesday, 11:40 a.m., courtyard, Pinedale High School

DARIA

All the girls,
around me
sit on my bench.
It smells like friends.

All of them
around me,
pretty clothes,
long hair.

All of them,
around me.
Some say names.
Some don't.

All of them,
around me
say things,
ask questions.

All of them
around me,
wait to see
what
I say.

ALEX

"I saw him at school today."

It's Jennifer. It's barely three, so she must have come the minute school got out. She has her uniform on, and this time the barrettes are white, instead of red. I wonder if she ever wears one white, one red. She holds out two books she brought me. The covers look a little girly, but I know I'll read them anyway.

"Saw who?" Though I know. Doctors have been in and out all day. They say I seem better, maybe well enough to go home tomorrow, that the cuts were just surface things, and it's good I drove away when I did. I tell them I don't feel well enough to talk to the police. I don't, actually. I've spent all day thinking about what to do about Clinton. I still don't know.

"Clinton. I can't believe he had the nerve to go to school. I saw him at lunch and told him what I thought of him."

"You shouldn't have done that."

"Why not? After what he did, he should be in jail, not school."

I should tell her the truth about Clinton, but I don't. They've been sticking me with needles all morning, and Mom was here, hovering and worrying I'd catch pneumonia or something just by being in this place. I don't think Mom trusts the doctors here.

Now she went to school to get my sister. She let Carolina go after her principal promised she'd keep an eye out. But Mom's still scared to let her walk home by herself.

"You just shouldn't have," I say.

"I couldn't help myself. I hate him. And you shouldn't have to deal with that crap—I was thinking last night that I would hate to be you."

That makes me mad. She's all proud of having told Clinton off, like I'm some weakling whose lunch money she got back from a bully. But I remember her shying away from my hand yesterday. Yeah, I remember that.

"Well, gee, thanks. Yeah, I was thinking you might prefer being someone else too. Maybe Kendall Barker."

"I didn't mean it that way."

"What *did* you mean?"

"I just meant, you have this horrible disease, and it's not even your fault."

"Fault?"

"Well, I mean, because of the transfusion."

I think of what Mom said yesterday, about how it matters to people. "Would it be different, if I got it some other way?"

"You mean if you were — ?"

Gay? I almost laugh, considering some of the fantasies I've been having about her.

I say, "If I got it shooting drugs or something? Would it matter that much? Would it be okay that I'm sick then?"

I see her eyes dart to my arm, looking for railroad tracks, and back. "No. No, of course it wouldn't matter. What matters is you're sick. I just meant it might make a difference to some people around here."

"People like Clinton?" *And you?*

"Right."

I take pity on her. "I don't shoot smack," I say. "And I'm not gay. It's not only a gay disease."

"I know that."

"But it shouldn't matter either way."

"It doesn't. Of course it doesn't."

Except that I can tell by looking at her that it does.

"You have this big, awful thing to deal with. And then, on top of it, you have to deal with people being so mean to you, like Clinton."

"The problem with the world isn't Clinton. Screw Clinton. What really sucks is the people who aren't like Clinton, the people like you."

The second I say it, I'm sorry. But it's out there now, and there's nothing I can do to reel it back in.

"What's that supposed to mean?"

I have to keep going. "People like you, you act all nice

and say hello to me in the hall or whatever, and then you feel like you did your good deed for the day because you were nice to the sick kid. But that doesn't mean you're going to invite me to your house or hang with me. You were never friends with me before this happened, and you won't be friends with me once it's over."

She's staring, but it's all coming out of me now, and I keep going and going like that bunny on the TV commercial.

"No one outside my family even touches me anymore, no one hugs me. You tell yourself you can't get sick from touching me, but you won't. One of the things they always tell terminals like me is, Be normal. Live for today. Seems like a pretty obvious concept, since I have no tomorrow. But the problem is, I have no today, either. People like you won't let me be normal. It makes you feel good to feel sorry for me. You can tell yourself you're not like Clinton, but you are."

Jennifer's standing there, her cheeks turning red like I slapped her. I guess I did. I start to say something else, I don't know what. Something else stupid, probably. She turns and walks out, still holding the books she brought me.

I am Freddy Krueger.

CLINTON

"Mr. Eutsey will be with you in a moment," the reception-ist says. "He's on a conference call."

"Thank you." Mom looks at her hands.

We've been sitting in the lawyer's office for fifteen min-utes now, not saying anything. Mom doesn't look at me. She hates me. I have a pencil in my hand. I want to bite it. I can't really explain about pencil biting. It's just something I did till lately, when my friends started making fag jokes about it. It's not that it tastes good or anything like that. It's just that sometimes, I feel like I . . . have to. But I've given that up. I don't do that anymore. So instead I jab my arm with the lead.

It hurts. But you know how, when something hurts, making something *else* hurt gets your mind off it? That's what I'm doing now.

"This would be a good time to tell me where you were yesterday," Mom says.

"I can't."

Jab. Jab. Jab.

"Oh, Clinton."

"I'm sorry."

Mom called Dad last night. I heard her on the phone, leaving a message on his answering machine. This morning, when I asked whether he called back, she shook her head. I heard her calling again after that.

Part of the reason I don't want to tell Mom I was out calling Dad yesterday is, I don't know if he'd even remember it. It's sort of embarrassing to say that, but there it is.

"Mr. Eutsey will see you now." The receptionist leads us into a fancy conference room with a big table. We take our seats. Then Mr. Eutsey comes in.

"Adele, how nice to see you," he says. "How are you?"

"I've been better, Bernard." There's a tremor in my mother's voice, and I look at her.

"Well, let's see if I can help you out."

Mr. Eutsey is the biggest black guy I've ever seen, maybe six-five, with a voice like James Earl Jones, who played Darth Vader in the *Star Wars* movies. If I saw him coming at me on the football field, I'd hide behind the Gatorade. Mom knows him 'cause she works for a judge. This must be the lawyer Dad was so afraid of. I can see why this guy could be scary. He's scaring me.

"Why don't you tell me what happened?" he booms.

"You've probably read about it in the paper," Mom says.

"Of course. But I was interested in hearing Clinton's

story. For example, where he was when all this happened. The best thing we can do is establish an alibi."

"I was home," I tell him, and Mom raises an eyebrow. I bet she thinks that since I lied so easy, I could lie about other things. "In bed," I add. *Jab, Jab, Jab.*

"Unfortunately," Mom adds, "I was asleep then. But I believe my son when he says he didn't do it."

Mr. Eutsey shrugs. "If mamas' believing won cases, not one of my clients would ever go to jail." He tents his fingers in front of his big face and looks over them at me. I wonder how many of his clients *are* in jail. "Clinton, this is a very serious charge."

"I know. But I didn't do it. I never touched the little fag. I mean, I'd never do that." I stop. Mom is giving me a hard look.

"That's not a word we use around here, boy," Mr. Eutsey says.

It takes me a second to realize he means *fag.* I feel my whole body getting hot and almost sweating. I mean, I know that to some people, that word is bad. But my friends use it all the time, even with people you don't think are actually gay. I hadn't even realized I'd said it.

"Sorry," I mumble.

"I apologize, Bernard." That's Mom. "Sometimes my son doesn't think."

"Not thinking can get you in trouble." He looks at me. "As I was saying, it's a serious charge. Because the boy is HIV-positive, this may be treated as a hate crime under Florida law. That means tougher penalties if you're convicted. It means jail."

"But I'm not like that. I don't hate him." But even as I say it, I'm wondering if I *am* like that. Because if I wasn't in trouble for what happened to Crusan, I know I wouldn't *mind* that it had happened. I might even have laughed about it.

"And, of course," Mr. Eutsey continues, "if the boy takes a turn for the worse, there could be other charges as well."

Other charges? I remember what that Jennifer girl said about Crusan dying. Could I get charged with murder? I look down at my arm. It's red, and I can see blood through the pieces of skin. I don't even feel it.

"I was calling my dad yesterday," I blurt. I'm looking at Mom. "I went to a pay phone because I didn't want Mom to know. I call him Monday mornings to make sure he makes it to work on time. He . . . drinks weekends."

"Oh, Clinton," Mom says. But I can see by the look on her face she's not mad at me. She's sort of feeling sorry for me—which is worse.

"Excellent," Mr. Eutsey says. "Where was the call made?"

"Gas-n-Sip on East Main. They're open early."

"That puts you right near the crime scene." Mr. Eutsey frowns.

"But I wasn't there when it happened. I rode my bike down East Main; I saw that retard girl. But Crusan wasn't there when I passed by."

Mr. Eutsey is dialing. He speaks into the intercom.

"Sandra, can you call the Gas-n-Sip on East Main. Tell them we're looking for some surveillance tape from yesterday around six a.m. . . . Yes, thank you." He looks at me. "The footage is stamped with the date and time. If we can get it, we may be able to establish that Clinton was elsewhere at the time of the assault."

"But if it wasn't the exact time, wouldn't that show that he was near the crime scene when it happened?" That's my mother. "That could hurt more than help."

"We need to take one thing at a time." Mr. Eutsey looks at Mom. When she nods, he says, "And, of course, your ex-husband would be able to corroborate the length of the phone call."

"If he remembers. I've called him five times since this happened because I suspected Clinton's absence might have something to do with him. He hasn't returned my calls. My ex-husband was once a respected businessman. But sometimes Jim would go on a bender and not come around for a week. When that happened, his family, his children, were meaningless."

I remember my dad's angry, crazy voice on the phone yesterday. My mother reaches across the table to pat my hand. I grab hers.

I can't believe she called him five times already, and he hasn't called back.

"Mr. Eutsey?" the voice on the intercom says. "I

spoke with Mr. Allen at Gas-n-Sip. They said the tape would have been erased. They only keep them twenty-four hours."

My arm is throbbing, and I feel tears clogging up my head. I screwed up, screwed up big-time. Mom squeezes my hand hard, and the only thing in the whole world that feels good is having her believe in me again. Which sucks, because I know I may kill it by telling the rest of the story. About the rock. I don't want to.

"Okay, minor setback," Eutsey says. "There will be other things we can do if charges are filed—subpoena the phone records to show the call to your ex-husband, for one."

If charges are filed. Subpoena. I see my life stretching before me like one long hell of reading in the cafeteria. Or worse, jail. I almost envy Crusan. Mom squeezes my hand again. She believes me. She said she believes me. I squeeze back, hard. Even though I know it will kill everything, I say, "There's something else I need to tell you."

Tuesday, 6:00 p.m., Bickell residence

DARIA

> *Mac and cheese*
> *for dinner.*
> *I like*
> *to say*
> *macncheese*
> *macncheese.*
>
> *Kids at school say,*
> *Macncheese.*
> *Mama says,*
> *Macaroni and cheese.*
>
> *"Makes*
> *me happy,"*
> *I say*
> *to Mama.*
>
> *"What does?"*
> *she says.*

"Macncheese."
I point.

Mama smiles.
She gives
me some.
I taste
orange
lumps
on my tongue.

"Makes
me sad,"
I say
to Mama.

"What?"

"Get
get confused."

"About what?"
Mama looks
worried.

"School.
Girls talk.
Can't
remember."

"Remember
what?"

"Names.
All the names."

"That's okay.
You can ask
again."

I think.
"And another."

"What?"

"Not sure.
Clinton
Clinton
Clinton
Didn't see
see him
Breakawindow."

"You mean
with the rock?"

"No.
Other.
Baseball bat."
The words
are hard
to know.

"I don't
not
sure."

Mama
doesn't answer.

"Sorry,
Mama."

Tuesday, 7:00 p.m., Memorial Hospital

ALEX

Mom walks in with two cops.

It's seven o'clock, four hours since Jennifer came and I told her off. She hasn't been back. Big surprise. I know she must have been in this area. She probably even had a break, but she hasn't stopped by. I need to face the fact that she isn't going to. I screwed up with her. I remember the story she told me about her dad. That's not the kind of story you tell everyone. She reached out to me, and I slapped her down.

"Alex, I'm Officer Reed, and this is Officer Bauer. We're here to talk about what happened yesterday." He's sort of squat and, when he talks, he doesn't look right at me or get too close. *Are you scared of me, little police officer?*

"I told the doctor I didn't feel well enough," I say instead.

"Your mother said it was all right." Officer Bauer steps closer and looks at my dinner tray, chicken breast with no skin, mixed veggies, mashed potatoes, pudding, and milk and says, "Looks like they have you on normal food anyway."

I grimace. "If you can call this normal food." But HIV

127

does weird things to your sense of taste, so I left picky eating behind months ago.

Reed speaks again. "It will just be a few questions. We're investigating the crime against you."

Yeah, I got that.

"I didn't really see the guy, not well enough to ID him." I feel a twinge when I say it. I saw the guy well enough to identify him as *not* Clinton Cole. He was thinner and had darker hair. I saw him well enough to know I'd never seen him before. Pinedale's a small school, maybe four or five hundred students. I know all that.

But it's so much easier to let it be Clinton Cole. A victimless crime, really, because Clinton's guilty of a bunch of other crap. This will get him off the street, not to mention off *me*.

Officer Bauer's talking again. The other officer still hangs back, like he doesn't want to get too close. "Sometimes if you talk about what happened, details come back to you that maybe you'd forgotten before. Sort of like people who remember witnessing a crime by seeing it reenacted on *America's Most Wanted*."

Or maybe they're just making stuff up.

From across the room, the other cop says, "Why don't you tell us what happened, son, what you remember?"

Why don't you come closer, and I'll tell you.

But Officer Bauer says, "We're trying to help you, son."

"Alex . . ." Mom says. "Just tell what you know."

So I tell them. I tell them about driving, about seeing Daria and the baseball bat and about how the glass didn't start flying right away, that the window was just cracked, but then it shattered on the second or third blow of the bat. "So I crawled onto the floorboard. That's why I didn't see much." I tell them about how I drove away even though I was a little worried about hitting a dog or something because I couldn't see. I tell them things that don't matter at all, things that are just in my head for no reason. I tell them everything, everything except the physical description of the guy who attacked me, the face in the mirror. That, I don't tell them.

"That's it," I say.

Officer Bauer looks disappointed. He says, "Your attacker, you didn't see his face at all?"

I look at him and shake my head. I feel so sleepy. I bet if they left, I could go right to sleep now with no Nick at Nite or anything. I yawn.

The officers close their notebooks. My mother smiles at me. She's happy I didn't tell them the truth, that I decided to fry Clinton Cole even if it means letting the really guilty guy go. She's so sure that it's Clinton and I'm mistaken. I realize that in the months since I was diagnosed, her pain and fear and anger have become so huge, they've taken over, and it's all about Us versus Them. I know she loves me. But somehow, what I stand for is almost as important as the fact that I'm her son.

Maybe that's how she deals—I don't know.

"Thank you, ma'am." Officer Bauer shakes my mother's hand. Neither cop shakes mine. Big surprise. "We'll be in touch if there are any new developments."

"Excuse me."

I'm surprised to hear my own voice. Everyone turns back, surprised too, like they'd forgotten for a moment there was anyone in the bed.

"Could I maybe . . ." I stop. It sounds like a request, and it's not one. Not really. "I have to talk to Clinton Cole."

CLINTON

Mom always says it's never good news when the phone rings after nine. According to her, most people know that you're not supposed to call that late. So if someone does call, it's either because they're rude or clueless or because somebody died. Or it was Dad, calling because the bartender hid his keys.

My friends pretty much always call whenever they feel like it, which is what Mom means by rude and clueless. But my friends are MIA today, so when the phone rings at ten, I wonder who died.

A few minutes later, Mom knocks on my door.

"That was Bernard . . . Mr. Eutsey."

Mom told the police and the newspapers they should call my lawyer about anything for my case. Now she says, "Bernard just got off the phone with the police. Apparently Alex Crusan told them he wanted to talk to you."

Shit.

"Do I have to go?" I don't want to. Aside from the obvious reasons of not wanting to be in the same room with the guy, particularly with open wounds, I also don't want to see

131

him when I know he thinks I'm scum. Mom says she's trying to understand about my throwing the rock. She knows I went a little crazy over Melody going there. But I don't think Crusan will be as understanding. I know I wouldn't be if my sister got hurt.

"Bernard was a little concerned that you might say something wrong. But we decided it could be a good idea. Bernard thinks maybe if Alex talked to you, it would jog his memory about what happened, that it wasn't you."

"What if he hates me so much he doesn't care either way?"

"Alex has said that he wanted to talk to you without police present. It wouldn't be a statement to the police, just a conversation. They have agreed that nothing in the conversation will be used against you."

"Then why does he want to talk to me?" I'm thinking anything could happen without the police there. I mean, what if he bit me or something? Part of me knows that's crazy, but why does he want to meet me? Or what if I screw up and say something really stupid?

"I don't know, Clinton. I think we have to wait and see. Maybe you can . . ." She stops, looks down.

"What?" I say.

"Clinton, you need to connect with this boy some-how. You have to make him see that you couldn't do something like this."

"Do you believe I couldn't?"

She looks at me a second before saying, "I believe you didn't do this. And I hope maybe you couldn't do anything like that ever."

I nod. I know I have to go.

Tuesday, 10:06 p.m., Daria's room

DARIA

> *Wait.*
> *Wait.*
> *Mama says*
> *wait.*
>
> *Maybe*
> *Alex Crusan*
> *saw better.*
> *He will*
> *tell.*
> *Maybe.*
>
> *Mama says*
> *she is not*
> *sad*
> *I saw it,*
> *said it*
> *wrong.*

I wish
I knew
the right thing.

A L E X

In that play *Rent*, that we saw in New York, the main character's a songwriter with HIV. He's trying to write the perfect song, one perfect song before he dies. One blaze of glory, he says.

I like that idea of doing something special, something to be remembered by. I don't know what that is for me yet. Not that it's critical now. I'm living, not dying. Living, not dying. That's what I'm telling myself every day. Except when I can't.

I don't know why that's what I'm thinking about while I wait for Clinton Cole to show his face here.

I don't even know why I wanted to talk to Cole. My parents, Mom especially, think it's a terrible idea, but I insisted, and the cops said okay. I guess I hope if I see Cole, if I look into his beady blue eyes, I'll know what to do. I'll know if he's the type of guy who'd do something like this, even if he didn't *this* time, or if he's some regular, normal asshole who's in way over his head. Maybe it shouldn't make a difference. Maybe I should just go along like Mom says, let him take the rap. But it's easy to say things don't make a difference, like trying to say being sick doesn't matter. It's harder to believe it.

Someone's at the door. I turn, expecting Cole.

It's my mother. "Alex, you do not have to do this."

"You already mentioned that."

"Then why—"

"Please, Mom, I appreciate everything you're saying, really. But you have no idea what it's like to live my whole life with other people deciding stuff for me."

"You are a child."

"I've grown up fast. I'm asking you to trust me to decide this one thing. The police think it's okay."

She looks at me. It's so quiet here. I'm going home tomorrow, but everyone thought it would be better to meet Cole here—neutral ground and all. And security. But I'm wearing regular clothes—khakis and a T-shirt that says "AIDS Project Florida 5K Run/Walk"—and sitting on the bed.

"I am only afraid for you to get hurt again," she says.

"Everyone's parents worry about that."

"But you are different."

"I don't want to be different. Don't you understand?" I meet her eyes. "Look, I know I made mistakes. I know I've given you plenty of reason to worry about me, to be disappointed." She knows I'm not talking about sneaking out on Monday anymore. I'm talking about having HIV in the first place. "But I'm asking you to trust me even though I haven't always given you reason to. I'm asking you to forgive me and let me try and move on."

We stand there a second, looking at each other, and I feel like for once, she really sees me. She knows what I'm talking about. Finally she sighs and walks over to my bed. "There is nothing to forgive you for."

I look at her like, *really*? She hugs me. I hug her back, hard.

After she leaves, Clinton Cole walks in.

I know he had to walk by the cops to get to me. They're in the hall in case there are problems. I didn't want them close enough to listen in, though. I wanted to be able to talk for real. After a little argument, they agreed.

Clinton stares at me, and if I didn't know him better, I'd say he looks sorry. Maybe. But I don't have to remind myself to hate this guy. I remember his crap in the cafeteria and in class. I remember the notes. I remember the rock. I remember everything.

"Wow," he says finally.

"*Que?*" I ask, because I know the Spanish will bug him. I can't resist.

"Nothing." He puts his hands behind his back. "Sorry. It's just . . . wow." He stares at my face, the bandages, but he doesn't come closer. I wonder if he thinks I'll attack him, or bite him. I fight this incredible urge to lunge at him, just to hear him scream.

"Those cops listening?" he says finally.

"They're just here in case something goes wrong.

They're not close enough to hear."

"Glad you're so sure."

I shrug. "Check."

"I don't need to do that." He says it loud. Then he tiptoes to the door and looks outside. He comes back. "Coast's clear . . . unless you're wearing a wire. I mean, if this is to get me to confess something, you should know I won't, 'cause I've got nothing to confess. I didn't do it."

"I'm not wearing a wire. You can check for yourself if you want."

"No thanks, man. I don't want to touch you." He holds out his hand, like to ward me off. Even from a distance, I can see he has these red welts on his arm. It looks like he stabbed himself with something. *Football Jock Involved in Bizarre Self-Mutilation Ritual.* Weird.

"No offense," he adds.

"None taken. I don't want you touching me, either . . . No offense." I untuck my T-shirt and lift it so he can see my stomach and chest. There's a few bandages and scratches, but no stitches and no wires. "Look."

Clinton doesn't move, but I can tell he's looking. I turn so he can see my back.

"You can pull that down now." He shakes his head. "Whoever it was really did a job on you."

"Yeah. Whoever it was did."

He holds both hands up. "It wasn't me, man."

"Sure."

"It wasn't. I mean, maybe you thought it was. Maybe

I can see why you could think that, but it wasn't."

"*Can* you see why I'd think it was you?" I'm still trying to figure out if he could have done it, even if he didn't do this. If he could have, maybe it's the same as if he did. Maybe it doesn't matter.

"I'm not following what you mean."

"You've done a lot of other stuff. Why should I believe you didn't do this? Why would anyone believe you, Cole?" I know he didn't do it, but I want to see him squirm. I hate him for all the stuff he's done to me since I've been here. I hate him for scaring my family, too. I want him to at least think about that for once. "Everyone's sure you did it because they all know what a raging asshole you are. Everyone."

When I say "everyone," Clinton's face changes, and I know I've hit a nerve. He turns away and walks to the door again and looks out, but I know it's just for something to do this time. He stands by the door a long time, and I sit there, quiet, feeling my face hurt. Finally he comes back.

He says, "Look, I know I wasn't nice to you, but . . ." He gestures at me. "This was over the line. I wouldn't do that." He takes a breath, a shaky one, and looks away. "You've got to believe me. My parents—they split up last year, and my mom's trying her best with us, but this is killing her. I don't expect you to care about me, but you know my mom. And my sister, Melody. They're good people. Probably I'm not a good person, but I'm not . . .

I wouldn't do this. Cutting someone up. A baseball bat—shit—maybe I'm a jerk, but I'm not an animal. I didn't do this. I didn't—"

"I know you didn't."

I don't know why I say it. I was planning on playing with him, toying with him awhile to see what he'd do. But when it comes down to it, I can't. He's there, practically blubbering, talking about his mom, and it makes me think of my own family, my parents. Clinton's still going, but when I say that, he stops. He looks at me.

"Huh?"

"I know you didn't do it," I say. "I saw the guy who did this. It wasn't you."

His face breaks into a big, doofy grin like he'd kiss me if . . . well, if he wasn't him and I wasn't me.

"That's great." He points toward the door. "Did you tell them?"

I shake my head no. "I said I wanted to talk to you."

"About what?" His smile begins to fade.

"Cole, you've been hounding me since the first day I walked into school. You left notes in my locker. You threw rocks at my house. My family's afraid to go outside because of you. You bother me every chance you get, and I'm sick of it."

"Look, man, I'm—"

"Sorry. Right. For now, so I'll tell the cops it wasn't you." Clinton's looking at the door again. "They can't hear us. I can take you down. I have every reason to let you rot in jail and get you off my back."

"Would you do that?"

"I want to. I really want to."

"It wouldn't be right."

"What about this is right? I know you threw the rock at my house. Daria doesn't make stuff up, and she couldn't have known that if you didn't do it. You did it. You hurt my sister, hurt all of us. But they'll give you a hand slap for that. You think that's right?"

"I don't know."

I don't say anything. He paces across the room, then comes back. "No. No, it wasn't right. It was a crummy thing to do. I didn't want to hurt Carolina. She's a sweet kid."

"But you wanted to hurt me?"

"No. I didn't want to hurt anyone. But I didn't want to get hurt, either. I wanted you out of here. I don't hate you. It wasn't personal, but I didn't want to sit by you in class. I didn't want to get AIDS."

I nod. "I didn't want HIV, either. But you can't catch anything, being in class with me."

"How can you be sure, though?"

"You get HIV from blood, from sharing needles or from sex. I've never met one person who got it any other way. They do studies about it, with scientists. It's not on toilet seats or chairs or pencils."

He looks at me. "How'd you get it, Crusan? From a transfusion like they said?"

The way he asks it, it's not mean for once, just curious. I almost want to tell him the truth. If I did, I know he'd believe me about everything. But I also know he'd tell everyone. I'm not sure Mom and Carolina are ready for that. I can't make that decision for all of us yet.

"You get HIV from sex," I repeat, avoiding his question but not his eyes. "Sex or blood. No other ways. You can't get sick from being in class with me. Understand?"

He looks away. I think about that blaze of glory again, and I think maybe that's not what it's about after all. Not something like a song or a home run record or even a debate title. Maybe it's all about how you live your life, about being human. And suddenly, I know I'm not going to let the police go on thinking Clinton did it. If I did that, I would be no better than Clinton is.

I have to let him go. I will let him go, but I want him to understand.

He still hasn't answered, so I repeat. "I can't get you sick, man. God, you think I'd want to go to school here if I could get people sick? You think I'd even be around my family?" I want him to . . . see me, Alex. Just Alex. I want someone to see me, even if it's Clinton. "I just want to be—a regular person until I can't be anymore. You need to believe me. Get it?"

He looks at me for a long time, like maybe the big behemoth is actually *thinking.* Finally he nods. "I get it."

I feel like I'm practically shaking. At least, I'm trying pretty hard not to. When I look at Clinton, maybe he is too.

I hold out my hand.

"Go ahead," I say. "Nothing will happen."

He doesn't move. Part of me's loving it, this ability I have to make him sweat. But I need him to shake my hand for real, not because he has to.

So I keep holding it out. I'm wondering whether I should just *not* push it. He said he understands. Maybe that's enough. I know I could get him to do whatever I want, just by threatening to tell them he did it. But I don't want that. I want him to believe me. So I don't say anything.

Finally he takes my hand.

CLINTON

His hand's not bleeding or nothing, so probably it's okay. It's not like I have much choice in the matter. I mean, if I shake his hand, there's this little chance I might get AIDS. But if I don't come to some kind of understanding with this guy, there's like a 100 percent chance I'm in deep shit. And even the school nurse said AIDS gets in through blood and . . . well, fluids, so if you aren't swapping any, you should be fine. At least, that's what I'm telling myself now. I'd feel better with gloves, but it's probably okay. It's okay. It's okay. So I do it.

His handshake is firm and dry and somehow, I know it's okay. I wonder what made me tell Crusan that junk about Mom and Dad. I never told my so-called friends that. I sort of thought Crusan might understand, might even know something about disappointing parents. I wonder again if he really got AIDS from a transfusion. I don't think so.

But asking again would be a deal breaker, so I keep it zipped.

It's like this special I saw on the Discovery Channel once (okay, it was Mel who watched it, but Dad and I were

145

in the room, playing blackjack) about lepers. That was this real bad disease where people's body parts fell off. It was in the Bible. They used to think it was a curse from God—like some people think about AIDS now, I guess, like people deserved it because of something they'd done. And they put them in special places so other people couldn't get it. But it turned out you couldn't get it from someone who had it. Dad said he wouldn't want to hang with them anyway, and I agreed with him then.

But now I'm thinking maybe Dad was wrong about things. A lot of things. I mean, it's been three days, and he hasn't returned a stinkin' phone call. He said Mom didn't want him involved with us—but I heard her, calling and calling, and he hasn't called back. Man, this was important. If I was with him, and not Mom, I might be in jail now.

Jail.

I let go of Crusan's hand. I start to wipe my palm on my jeans. I stop myself when I realize he's looking at me. *Stupid.*

I say, "Sorry, man."

He shrugs. "We don't have to be friends." I can hear in his voice that he doesn't want to be friends with me anyway.

"What do you want from me then?"

He looks down. "Nothing." He shakes his head. "I don't want anything from you."

"But you're going to tell them it wasn't me, right?" I

don't get this guy. He dragged me here for—what? Just to chat?

He nods. "I'll tell them it wasn't you that morning. And the other stuff, the rock and the notes in my locker and stuff . . ." He shrugs. "I guess we'll see what happens."

"You want me to confess, don't you?"

I sure don't want to. Mr. Eutsey said they might not believe Daria, on account of her being retarded. So I don't have to confess anything. Not unless that's part of Crusan's deal for telling them I didn't do Monday. I still don't get what his deal is.

"You don't have to," he says.

"But you must want something from me?"

He thinks about it. "Well, yeah, there's one thing."

"What is it?" *Shit. What is it already?*

"Just leave my family alone, okay? My mom, she wants to leave town over this. I hate it here, but we can't afford to leave. I can't make you stop it, but would you . . . just be decent, huh?"

I nod. I know that now that I've talked to the guy, face-to-face, man to man, I couldn't go shoving secret notes in his locker anymore anyway. It's hard to explain, but once you look someone in the eye like that—I mean, *really* look at them—it's like you can't *not* look at them again. You can't not see them. It was a stupid thing, throwing that rock. Stupid, and mean, too. I know that now.

"I'll tell them I threw the rock." Even as I say it, I'm thinking, *Are you nuts, man?*

"I said you don't have to."

"I know I don't have to, but I will. I just . . . I want to get it over with. I want this over. And . . ."

I don't finish. What I'm thinking is something like, I want to make it right. He was decent when he didn't have to be. I want to be decent too.

He examines my face, then gestures at the door. "Then why don't you go get those cops in here?"

I do.

Wednesday, 10:30 a.m., Mrs. Taub's office, Pinedale High School

DARIA

Mama says,
it is fine.
Alex Crusan saw.
Alex Crusan
knew.

Not Clinton
who hurt Alex.
But Clinton
threw
the rock.
They know that
because of
me.

Mama says
I am still
a
hero.

Wednesday, 11:00 a.m., Memorial Hospital

ALEX

After Clinton and the cops leave, I go into the bathroom. I want to see my face in the mirror. The verdict: could be worse. The cuts look pretty scary, and it will be another week before I can get the stitches out. I won't go to school until then. If it was up to Mom, I'd never go to school, but we compromised on this.

When I was a kid, I was in the hospital once with pneumonia. I cried the whole time. I missed school, missed my friends. I wanted to get out.

These past two days, I've hated being here, but not because I missed anything on the outside. So far I've had nothing on the outside. But I want to now.

I go back to my bed and press the button for the nurse. When she shows up, I ask her, "I'm sorry to bother you about this but . . . will I have scars all over my face?" This is suddenly intensely important to me.

She looks at me a second, then says, "Didn't the doctors tell you about taking care of yourself?"

They might have, but I might not have been paying attention.

"I'm not sure," I say.

She rolls her eyes. "What you want to do, hon, is wear a hat and use suntan lotion—SPF thirty, at least, every time you leave the house for the next few months. Six months to be safe. Then you should be okay. Maybe you'll have some little marks, but they won't show to anyone who doesn't know they're there, you know? Nothing worse than a pimple, hon."

I nod. "Thank you."

"Hey, you're a good-looking boy. Gotta take care of yourself, right?"

Much later, I turn out the light and lay back for my last night in the hospital bed. It's only nine, but for once, I'm ready to go to sleep. Today was a good day. I feel like, maybe, I actually got through to Clinton. I made him understand. Maybe he'll even tell his friends. Maybe.

Okay. Doubtful about telling his friends. But I know that talking to Cole did something for *me*.

But I know that I have to talk about what happened to me. And to do that, I'd have to tell the truth about how I got sick. It shouldn't be that big a deal—it's nothing that earthshaking. Except that Mom and Dad have been going with that Ryan White/Innocent Victim transfusion story for so long that it *seems* like a big deal. It seems like they're ashamed of me, is how it seems.

I push the thought out of my head. My mother said she isn't mad at me, and I have to believe that.

I turn on the light and sit up. Maybe this won't be an easy night like I thought it would be.

How My Life Changed Forever by Alex Crusan

This whole thing started because Austin Ionata's older brother knew how to get us into a college party.

It was the week after my sixteenth birthday. Austin and Danny and I were at Austin's house. We always hung there because Austin's parents were never around, never hovered over him, unlike mine, who'd follow you into the bathroom if they could get away with it. We'd stolen a bottle of vodka from the liquor cabinet and were playing Quarters. I never drank much, and I was sort of flying before the bottle was even half empty. So I was glad when Danny said, "Let's order a pizza. This is boring."

After Austin ordered the pizza, I called home to let them know I wouldn't be there for dinner. Austin's brother, Mike, who was a freshman at the university, came in when the pizza did.

"Hey, pizza." He opened the box and peeled off two slices. He folded them and shoved the whole mess into his mouth.

"Hey!" Austin said. "That'll be five dollars, please."

"Put it on my bill," Mike said. "Or better yet . . ." He finished wolfing down the two slices and peeled off another.

"Hey!" Austin said again.

Mike took a bite, doing a major cheese pull with it. "You want to go to a party?"

"A college party?" I said. "We couldn't go without ID."

"Nah—this one frat has all their parties off campus now. Makes it more . . . interesting without the campus police around."

So, of course, we were going. But, also, of course, I had to call home again. I told Mom I was staying over Austin's.

"Are his parents there?" she said.

"They always are."

A sigh. "Be careful, Alejandro."

"I always am."

When I hung up, Danny said, "It's so lame, you having to call your parents all the time, Crusan."

"Hey, Danny," I said, "ever think maybe your parents don't make you call because they don't care if you get home?"

Which shut him up.

The party was at an apartment complex near school. There were at least two hundred people there, spilling out of the building and into the parking lot. Some guy stopped us at the entrance. I wasn't really worried about passing for a college student. People always thought I was older because I was tall. But when the guy stepped in front of me and said, "Fifteen," I stopped.

"No, I'm . . ."

Mike nudged me. "He means fifteen dollars for the beer and stuff."

I wasn't sure I'd drink anything. I wasn't drunk anymore, but I felt sort of halfway there, halfway human, halfway alive. But I paid my fifteen dollars anyway, got a wristband, and followed my friends to the keg.

I got a beer and sipped it. My friends went off somewhere, gesturing to me to follow. But then a bunch of other people got between us, so I lost them.

It got darker, and people kept coming, and I held tight to my cup, which was sweating and half gone warm and funny tasting. Some people were dancing in the grass, and I saw Mike with some guys drinking out of funnels. The music was an electronic haze, hanging in the trees. People were moving in and out of their own shadows, and I knew I shouldn't be drunk. I hadn't even had very much. But I felt like when I was a little kid and sick, when you wake with these fever dreams and everything feels half real, half not. I could feel the pizza like it was clogging my head, in there with the music, and finally, the beer became too hot even to pretend to drink. I dumped it out, got another, and held the cold plastic cup to my forehead until it hurt. Then I thought, Maybe go ahead and drink it.

With the first sip of beer, I felt my stomach lurch. I went off into the bushes and puked, felt a little better, then puked some more and felt a lot better. I started looking for my friends, but everyone looked the same, all black and white, and the heat of the crowd brought the sickness back. I finally went and sat on the steps leading to the upstairs apartments. I figured I'd watch until one of them came by.

I heard a voice behind me.

"You can't sit here."

At first I wasn't sure she was talking to me. I didn't answer.

"Hey!" A hard tap on my shoulder. "You can't sit here, asshole. You're violating the fire code!"

This time I twisted to see where the voice came from. A girl. A tiny girl. In the gray haze from the party, I could make out her short haircut and that she was pretty. Her arms were loaded down with books.

"Did you hear me?" she said.

Finally I said, "Yeah, I heard you. I just . . ."

"Stupid frat boys, think you can party every night, sit anywhere you want whenever you want, think no one else has the right to study or sleep or anything."

"I'm not a frat boy," I said, sort of amazed she'd think I was old enough, this close. "This is my first frat party ever. My friends brought me, and now I lost them, and I was . . . You live here?"

"Right." Her voice was a little less hostile. She was a college student, nineteen, maybe twenty.

"I'm Alex."

"Leigh." She stared at the step. I was still in the middle of it.

"Oh . . . sorry." I scooted over an inch so she could pass. "Look, I needed to sit down a minute. I got a little sick, okay? I don't usually drink much, and I guess . . ."

She didn't move past me.

"It must suck, living here, having all this noise all the time." I considered my stomach. Better. Puking had helped. I didn't even feel drunk anymore. Or, at least, I didn't think I would if I could get away from the pounding, pulsating music that seemed to make my bones vibrate. Suddenly I wanted out of there more than anything.

"Look," I said, "can I carry your books upstairs? You look really loaded down."

She smiled for the first time. "That'd be great. I'm on the fourth floor, and those . . . idiots are trying to see how many people they can get into the elevators."

I stood and took her books from her, then waited for her to get ahead of me so I could follow her to her apartment.

"This is very decent of you," she said.

"Hey, I'm a decent guy."

"You're a minority, let me tell you. There's a shortage of guys who'll carry a girl's books. I don't know if I've ever met one before."

"Well, you've met one now. A card-carrying member of Book-Carrying Guys of America."

"Only member, maybe," she said, laughing.

We got to the third-story landing and stood there a

moment, looking out. The party spread across the apartment complex and, in the dark, the shapes of people looked like the bumps on a topographical map. The music was pounding, pounding, pounding.

"They really do this every weekend?" I asked.

"What?"

I repeated the question, louder. We were walking up the third flight now, and I was watching her from behind. She was smaller than girls I was usually into, but there was something about the way she moved and the very tininess of her that made me want to watch her, her short hair bobbing up and down, her tiny butt. I wanted to touch her, suddenly. Blanca, my girlfriend, would only let me touch her over her shirt. She wouldn't touch *anything* of mine. Said she didn't want to give me ideas.

"Yeah," Leigh said. "And sometimes, they party during the week too." She stopped and fumbled in her pocket for her keys. She turned and saw me staring at her. I glanced away. "I didn't mind so much, first semester. But I got sick during finals—major flu—and I need to make up all my exams, plus the new work, and it's ridiculous, having to go to the library all the time because I can't think straight here."

I looked at her again. In the clingy blue T-shirt she had on, I could tell she wasn't wearing a bra.

"You're a freshman then?" she said.

I nodded. I started to say my usual thing, about starting school late, so I was really too old to be a freshman.

Then I realized she meant a *college* freshman.

"And this is your first frat party."

"I guess I don't party much, either. I live at home." Changing the subject. "You'd think they'd have a little consideration."

"No one else in the building seems to mind. Guess I'm a nerd."

"Then I'm a nerd too."

We were walking toward her apartment. I looked over the railing. Downstairs, two guys wearing yellow raincoats even though it wasn't raining were shaking up beer cans and spraying each other's mouths. We reached her door, and Leigh unlocked it and gestured me inside. A girl's apartment. I placed her books on the loveseat near the door.

"Guess we should've known, huh?" she said. "'Suntan U,' they call it." She flipped a switch. I turned to look at her. In the light she was even cuter, even almost beautiful. Her hair was penny colored, blue eyes, and her skin was white, almost see-through, like she'd come from another world.

"No suntan for you."

She smiled. "Nope. I just burn." She looked at my arm, which was permanently brown, though baseball and beach season were long over. She touched it. "You fit right in here."

I felt a warm shiver run from my wrist to my shoulder even on the side she hadn't touched. I tried to laugh, but it didn't come out right. "Genetics," I said. "I was even a tan baby. And I play ball—so I'm outside a lot."

Her hand was still on my arm, so I knew it wasn't accidental; she wanted to touch me. "Not me. I'm not athletic at all. I was a debate team nerd in high school."

"No kidding? I . . ." I stopped. I knew the conversation would end if she found out how old I was. She thought I was in college, and now I was stuck with that. "I used to debate in high school too. Original oratory."

"Me too. Funny. We have a lot in common. I'm going to law school next year."

"So you're a senior then?"

"Yep, an older woman."

I glanced at the door, which had closed behind us. "Well . . ."

Leigh looked at me. "Well . . ."

"I guess . . ." I stopped. I was going to say I should go down and find my friends, but I didn't want to go. I looked around the room. It had what my mother would call a decor—blue and white, warm and inviting, neat except a mess of CDs on the floor. From outside I could still hear the pulsing music, but it was dulled by the door.

"Maybe—" We both started at the same time, then stopped.

"What were you going to say?" she asked.

"No. You first."

"I was thinking if you wanted coffee or something . . . it's not like I'm getting any sleep anyway."

"That'd be great." I didn't drink coffee, but I'd long since given up on Austin and Mike, and some inside voice was shouting, *You have a shot with this girl! A college girl!* "You mind if I use your bathroom?"

She gestured me toward it and went to the kitchen. I did the usual bathroom stuff and rinsed my mouth out. But I could still sort of taste the bile, so I started snooping in her cabinets, looking for mouthwash. I figured the party noise would cover the sound. I didn't find any, but I did find a round, plastic package which I knew (embarrassingly enough, from having seen one in my own parents' bathroom) was birth control pills. The package was open and some were missing. *I have a shot*, I thought, then wondered if she had a boyfriend. But he would be here, wouldn't he, on Saturday night? I put the pills back. No mouthwash. So I rinsed my mouth again and went back to the living room.

The living room smelled like coffee, and Leigh had moved the books off the loveseat. She was sitting at its center, waiting, looking at me.

"Coffee's not ready yet," she said.

"Should we put on some music?" I asked. "Maybe it would drown out the other stuff."

"Nice thought, however doubtful." She gestured at the CD pile. "Choose something."

I sensed it was a test. She had all types of music, some classical and jazz, but also some recent stuff and groups I'd never even heard of. I finally found an old

Smashing Pumpkins album. I put on my favorite song, "Through the Eyes of Ruby."

"Your innocence is treasure," the CD sang a minute later. "Your innocence is death."

"Good choice." She nodded her approval. She moved over, making a tiny amount of room for me between herself and the sofa arm. I sat. She was so close I could feel her, even though we didn't touch. "This is my favorite song. I love the lyrics. Like poetry."

"Yeah, mine too. I think the words are the most important thing about a song. Don't you?"

She didn't answer, just leaned close. I didn't think of Blanca at all. I knew I had to kiss this girl now if I was going to, so I did. Her lips were soft, and she tasted—somehow—like flowers. My hands went instinctively to her body, slipping under the blue T-shirt to touch her. I couldn't believe she let me, even pulled me closer, her hands in my hair. It was like there was nothing but touching her, her touching me. I sort of fell on her, kissing her, feeling fine now, feeling lost and tense and relaxed, and fine. So fine.

Then sirens. At first I thought they were in my head. Then I saw blue lights in the window, spinning, turning. The music outside stopped, and there was only ours. Leigh moved away.

"Hooray, South Miami Police," she said.

"What?"

"They're breaking it up." She glanced at her watch.

"Only one a.m. this time."

The song ended, and below I heard people running, yelling.

"My friends." I looked out the window. "I don't know if I have a ride home."

"I can drive you home." She put her hand on my shoulder. "But I thought maybe you'd stay."

I did stay that night, my first time. I knew it was safe because of the birth control pills. And when I left the next morning, I got her number. I called her. It wasn't a one-night stand. I wasn't a scum. Really, I sort of—I don't know—fell in love with her. But maybe I really didn't know anything about her. And she didn't know anything about me, either.

A few weeks later, she found out. Or she found out how old I was anyway. Then it was over. The way she yelled that last day, I knew I'd never see Leigh again.

And I didn't. I went on with my life. I kept going out with Blanca and getting crap from my friends for not getting laid. But that summer, I got a note from Leigh in the mail.

Get an AIDS test, it said. And, Sorry.

There was no signature.

Sometimes I wonder where she is, how long she'd had it, not knowing. I wonder what her family said, if she's still in college, if they still love her. And I wonder if she's sick.

When I found out, my mother cried a lot, and I didn't

want to get out of bed for about a week. Then I made myself. I didn't feel bad physically, but everything had changed. My parents didn't understand how I could have gotten it. I mean, they *did* understand, but they didn't want to. They hadn't raised me to have sex in high school. They'd preached about waiting. We'd never discussed condoms, but I knew anyway. Everyone knows. My mother told me not to tell anyone I had it, or if I did, to tell them I got it from a transfusion, which these days is pretty much impossible, medically. I don't know why, what the difference was. But I guess she didn't want people to think:

I'm gay.
I'm a junkie.
I'm a skank.
I deserve it.

Other than Mom and Dad, none of my relatives know the truth about how I got sick, not even Carolina or Aunt Maria, who told me I wasn't like those people in *Rent*. I know my parents are disappointed. But at least they've stood by me.

Most people assume I'm gay anyway, even when they hear I got it from a transfusion. I'm so over caring about that. It sounds dumb to say I didn't think it could happen to me. But I didn't. I didn't.

Wednesday, 6:00 p.m., Cole residence

CLINTON

Dad finally returned Mom's calls. He said I shouldn't have confessed to anything. If he'd been around, he wouldn't have let me.

There's really nothing to say to that, so I don't say it.

Mr. Eutsey says he can get me into something called a "diversion program" where nothing will be on my permanent record. That's something at least. I can't believe I could have screwed up my whole life over something like this. I can't believe I didn't think.

Even though I'll probably have probation with a million hours of community service, the hardest thing is telling Melody I threw that rock.

"But why would you do that?"

None of the answers sound right anymore.

"I don't know. I guess I was scared. I didn't want you over there, catching anything."

"But that's stupid. I couldn't catch AIDS from Alex. Not unless . . ." She makes a face.

"I'm sorry. I guess I'm stupid."

"You are. I lost my best friend, and it's all your fault."

She gives me a hard look. "I hate you."

She storms off to her room

It's a tough evening, with Melody not speaking to me and Mom fuming about Dad. There's all this silence around, and I'm starting to think you can be stupid, like dumb in school, and stupid, like dumb in life. I hurt the Crusans, even if I didn't hit anyone with a baseball bat. I know that. I don't like knowing it. But I don't want to be that guy anymore.

So at nine-thirty, I pick up the phone and dial 411. Then, the number.

"Who is this?" The voice on the other end doesn't have that much of an accent, really.

"Hello, Mrs. Crusan?"

"Who is this?" she repeats.

"It's Clinton. Clinton Cole."

A little gasp. "Do not bother us here. Can't you leave us alone?"

I hear her voice go farther away. I yell to keep her there. Mom, who's been working on legal papers of some kind, looks up when I say, "Please! Please don't hang up, Mrs. Crusan."

Mom's eyes lock on me, and she's like a tigress, ready to spring if I say the wrong thing. I remember she'd get that look around Dad sometimes. I can see now she worries she screwed up with me by staying with Dad so long, that maybe I'll turn out like him. But I'm not like Dad. I'm not. And I'm going to show her that.

I say, "I'm sorry, Mrs. Crusan. I wanted to say . . ." I turn away so Mom can't see my face. "I'm so sorry for what I did."

I hear the phone clatter onto the receiver.

I hang up the phone and stand there a minute. Then I walk over to the window. There's no moon out, and the sky's so black that all you can see are stars, stars for miles, going and going and going and never touching one another.

A minute later, I feel Mom's hand on my shoulder.

We just stand there, looking at the stars, and I'm glad she's there, still there. Always there.

Thursday, 7:45 a.m., Pinedale High School

DARIA

"What do you expect?"
The girl's voice
cuts
through me
in the hall.

"What do you expect?"
the boy behind me.
"She's a retard."
"Retard."
"Retard."

"How would she know?"
"Of course
she got it wrong."

I pretend
not to hear,
and after a while,
I do not.

I know
I did right.
I helped.
I did help.

What they say
doesn't matter.

I helped.

Their names
don't hurt me.

I helped.
I can help.

ALEX

Leaving the hospital, they make me ride down the elevator in a wheelchair. Hospital policy, they say. But I still hate it. Makes me think of that day at Disney World.

An orderly's pushing me, and Mom follows behind. Mom says she guesses I did the right thing, but she isn't real happy about it. I think what she's really upset about is the fact that they don't know who really did it. I am too. We're leaving early—around three—because Mom doesn't think it's safe to be out after dark. I actually agree with that, too. It's scary to think that there's still someone out there who did this, who hates me that much that he didn't care what happened to him, so long as he hurt me.

Mom wanted to leave even earlier, but I held out for three so I could look for Jennifer on the way down. Not obsessive at all, right?

I see her.

She's by the flower cart, like the first day I saw her, surrounded by roses and those big star-shaped pink flowers. The barrettes have totally given up, and her hair's in her face. She looks good. I wish she'd talk to me, though.

169

We're by the elevator. I stand, eliciting protests from Mom and the orderly. I walk over to her.

"Look, I'm sorry," I say. "I was a first-class jerk."

She looks, like, are you talking to me? Finally she says, "Yeah. You are."

I note her use of present tense. I say, "It's just . . . tough. Look, I won't be in school for about a week. But I'll be there next Wednesday. Will I see you there?"

She says, "Guess you will. It's a small building." She gestures over my shoulder. "Your elevator's here."

In the time it takes for me to turn and look, she pushes her flower cart away.

Friday, all day, Cole residence and Pinedale High School

CLINTON

Friday morning before school, the telephone rings, and Mom gives it to Mel.

When Mel gets off the phone, she says, "That was Carolina. She invited me to come over her house, but she can't come here because of Clinton." She gives me a mean look. "So that means I'll be over there more than ever," she finishes with a note of triumph.

"That's great," I say. I don't tell her about calling the Crusans. I don't know why I don't, except I don't want to act like I'm some big hero. I'm not a hero. I'm still not even sure I want Mel going over Carolina's house. I'm still not really sure it's safe, but I know it's going to happen. So I let it go.

At school the big news at school is they caught the guy who did it.

Davis McNeill was one of last year's seniors, a football player. He's got a younger sister, Brianna, who's a junior here.

Apparently McNeill's girlfriend caught him with

another girl, so she told the police that he'd said he'd "make that little homo sorry he came to Pinedale." The police didn't pay a whole lot of attention, figuring it was a little matter of "a woman scorned." But when Alex told them it wasn't me but it was a guy in a letter jacket, the police remembered. They took out a warrant to search Davis's apartment. He lives in a studio over his parents' garage . . . about a block from where Alex got attacked.

They found a baseball bat in the closet. It was a metal bat that had marks on it that looked like cuts from broken glass.

So everyone at school is talking to me again. Even Ms. Velez says hi. Mo and Andy ask me to sit at their table, and Alyssa sends me a note last period.

Rents say all clr 2 talk 2 u. R U coming to my party next Fri. nite?

I don't answer. I don't know what to say. So it kind of surprises me when I get her, live and in person, at the end of the period. She stops me at my desk

"Hey, Clint, didn't you get my note?"

"Um, sure."

"I thought maybe you were going to . . ." She looks down. "I mean, I hope you're not mad about me not talking to you. It was just my parents, you know?"

"Sure." Out of the corner of my eye, I see Brett, giving me a thumbs-up. I ignore him. "I mean, nah, I'm not mad at you. I understand about parents."

"Yeah, they're lame. I mean, I was totally on your side the whole time. I told people that."

"You mean you told people you thought I didn't do it?"

"Um, sure . . . well, and even if you had done it, it's not like it matters that much. I mean, my brother, Jake, was saying you were, like, a hero or something."

I look at her, a good look. Her eyes are still the same, and her fingers, and she's wearing that same pink shirt that always makes me want to touch her. Except today, I just don't. Don't get me wrong—she's really beautiful and all. Maybe I'll still ask her, or maybe not, or maybe I won't go. I mean, I'm glad I'm on the team and all, and I wouldn't go back to before, to the way I was as a kid, for anything. But back when I was a dorky fat kid, I used to spend a lot of time alone, and I used to know who I was. Lately I'm not so sure.

"Well, I guess I'm not a hero," I say, coming to. "Look, I have to get to class."

I wait and hold the door for her on the way out.

At lunch I sit with the guys, and I do everything the way I used to. They act like nothing's changed. Maybe nothing has for them. It's easier for me to go along. After all, it's not like I can up and find a whole group of new friends in this crummy school. But inside, that's where everything feels different. I don't know if it's because I'm mad at them for thinking I'd do something like that or because they dumped me so easy, just like that time at Wal-Mart. But they're the only friends I have, so I sit with them.

I wonder when Crusan will be back. Not that I want to hang with the guy or anything, understand. I just wonder.

Friday, 12:00 p.m., courtyard, Pinedale High School

DARIA

*No one
sits
with me today.
I
don't
care.*

*They don't
really like me.
People think,
I don't know.
But I do.*

*I ask
Mrs. Taub,
"Alex Crusan?
He'satschool?"*

*"Not yet."
Her mouth
frowns.*

"Miss him,"
I say.

"So do we all,"
she says.
"I mean,
so do I."

The following Wednesday, 7:15 a.m., Pinedale High School

ALEX

The first person I see when I go back to school Wednesday is Clinton Cole. He's getting out of a car with a bunch of other jocks as I park. He looks down when he sees me. He's embarrassed. Since I have to sit by the guy in class, I mutter, "Hey."

I unbuckle my seat belt and get out of the car.

My face still aches.

He mutters "Hey" back. So do his friends. They aren't exactly asking me to sit with them at lunch, but I wouldn't want them to. I'm just glad I did the right thing, especially since they caught the guy who really did it. I walk toward the school, alone.

The night I got out of the hospital, I had a long talk with my parents. I told them I wanted to start telling the truth about how I contracted HIV.

"I'm not going to take out a billboard or anything, but I'm not lying anymore. I can't go through life lying."

They both stared at me, stunned.

I hurried on before they could say anything. "And I think we need to tell Lina. I'm sure she's heard people talking. And it feels bad, being dishonest with her. She's my sister. She's not a baby anymore. Besides, don't you think it's better to know what's out there than to go through life stupid?"

I don't think they agreed with me, but they knew it was no use arguing. We told Carolina that night. I don't know when I'll tell other people, but it'll be soon. I'm tired of lying. I'm tired, and it doesn't help.

When I'm almost at the building, I see Daria. She's sitting on her bench, alone, as usual. When she sees me, her smile is like the Fourth of July. I wonder why anyone wouldn't be nice to someone like that when it takes so little to make her happy.

Then I wonder if that isn't exactly what I accused Jennifer of.

I don't have too much time to think about it because she comes bounding up to me, yelling, "Alex Crusan, you're back."

I grin at her. "In the flesh. I mean, yeah."

"Not Monday . . . no car."

It takes me a second to realize she means going to Dunkin' Donuts.

"No," I say. "My mother doesn't want me driving alone anymore. It's November, and it stays dark longer. She's afraid I'll get hurt. So we went Sunday night on the way to church and bought donuts and brought them home for Monday."

She nods. "My mom too . . ." A long pause. "Thinks I am a baby."

178

I shrug. "I bet it's not that. It's just, they want us to be safe." Daria's voice is really loud, and I notice a few people looking at us, walking by. The HIV kid and the Down Syndrome girl. Well, eat my shorts. Then I notice Jennifer's one of the ones looking. When I meet her eyes, she turns away. I tell myself I don't care.

"I like . . . pink box," Daria says, still loud.

"What?"

". . . for for donuts."

I understand now. "Yeah, I like the pink box too."

"Pink box like pink hair," she says.

I look down at her face, so happy to see me, and I want to just hug her. So I do.

When I let her go, I say, "Sometimes my little sister, Carolina, even gets pink donuts."

"I like pink donuts," she says, like she's not startled at all by my sudden hug.

Jennifer's gone. I say, "Thank you for telling them about Clinton, about the rock. It was a good thing to do."

She nods, happy, and the warning bell rings.

"Gotta go now," she says.

"Yeah, I do too," I say.

I don't see Jennifer the rest of the day. Thursday either, or Friday. This is more than weird because I used to see her around all the time, so she must be avoiding me. Plus there are only a few hundred kids at this school. You can't really avoid someone here. I tell myself I don't care. It wouldn't have worked, me and her. Why would she want someone like me? And besides, what else can I do? I've already apologized. When you apologize and someone doesn't accept, you have to stop, or it's stalkerish.

I see her Monday, but the late bell rings, and she starts running toward class. I tell myself I don't *think* she's running away from me.

Meanwhile, some people—a lot of people—are nicer to me. I mean, there's still people who obviously don't want to breathe air that's been up my nose, but other people have gotten nicer. So I have friends now—sort of—a place to sit at lunch, a partner for my science project, and an invitation to Alyssa Black's party Friday night (I've decided to go if my parents let me). Maybe they're not *all* bad. And maybe I didn't help either, by not really trying to get to know anyone. I saw them as all being the same. But isn't that the same as them thinking they knew about me, when they didn't?

Anyway, I talked to Mr. Bell, the debate team advisor, and told him I'd like to join. After all, I'm really good at debate. And this school needs me because their team is pretty lame.

Before I was HIV-positive, I was okay popular. I was good in sports, which is important, and people liked me. After, even in Miami, things changed a lot. I still had some friends, but there was this sense of being—I don't know—the resident oddity. Like, "Here's the trophy case and the auditorium, and here's the kid with HIV. Say 'Hi,' Alex." And even some of the friends I had, it was like they were making it a point to be friends with me, like it would go on their college app or something.

And that's how it still is here. But it's getting better. At least some people are giving me a chance. And I'm giving them one too. Maybe some people are only being nice because it's the cool thing now. But I hope I'll make some real friends too. It's good. If I'm going to live for today, I have to start by making friends, even in Pinedale.

Then Monday afternoon, I see her in the parking lot.

Her: Jennifer.

I know her car. It's a white Civic, and I don't see it anywhere. Yet there she is, standing there. I tell myself she's not here to see me.

She walks around the general area of my car, so I say, "Need a ride home?"

"Maybe."

She examines my baby, which has a new paint job and looks like nothing ever happened. Meanwhile, my face still hurts to the touch, and I slather it with SPF 30 every day. I reach for the door handle.

"You were right," she says.

"Right about . . . ?"

"What you said. It took me a while to admit it, but what you said about me was true, at least partly."

No! I don't want to be right about this! After she got so righteously indignant over what I said, I convinced myself I was wrong about her, that she really did like me as a person.

She says, "That probably was why I came to see you, at least part of it. I thought I was so much smarter than everyone else. I was going to be a doctor, so I knew better than those idiots. I was such a . . . You saw right through me."

I try and fix it. "But at least you came. No one else did."

"Right." She looks up at me. Her hair's loose, free from its ponytail, and it sort of flutters around her face like a bunch of butterflies. "But I came back because I liked talking to you."

"Yeah?"

"Yeah. I was always . . . interested in you, from the second you came here."

Interested? I nod. "Yeah, some girls are into guys with problems."

She smiles, smart-assy. "Oh, maybe that was it."

"Look, you don't have . . . you aren't required. I know I'm a tough sell. Most people don't even want to use the bathroom after me, much less—"

"I'm not sure what I want. But I like you, Alex. When you said that about wanting someone to hug you—I wanted to."

I'm drowning. I feel myself come up for air, but I'm drowning. I want to believe her, want to pick her up like in some movie and drive off into the sunset. But I remember what she said that day in the hospital, about it not being my fault, being positive. Would she see me differently if she knew the truth?

I say, "Um . . . really?"

"Yeah. I want to be friends. I want to be friends and maybe . . ."

"What?"

"I don't know. Friends, at least. To start with."

Maybe it's the novelty, the being able to say she was so liberal, so smart that she'd even hang out with me. Maybe when the novelty wears off, she'll bail. She'll probably bail.

Who cares?

"But what about . . . ?" *If I get sick? Or if people don't want to talk to you because you're with me?* "You don't need to get involved with someone like me."

Why are you arguing with her? A day, a week of being with someone is a lot better than nothing. I feel my aching face, and I think, Even hurting is good. Being hurt is at least being alive. Being real.

"I'm not worried about what people think, if that's what you're thinking. And I'm not worried about you getting sick. I mean, I don't want you to. But who knows what could happen? Maybe they'll discover a cure tomorrow. Maybe I'll get hit by a bus on the way home. Who knows?"

"Who knows?" I echo.

"You have to let people in," she adds. "Not be afraid of them."

"I know that. But . . ."

I stop. I know I have to tell her the truth about that one thing, tell her and hope it doesn't matter.

"You said you were lonely. You said you wanted someone to talk to. Why not me?"

Even if it's only a day, I'm ready for it. I nod.

"So, how about that ride?" I say.

"Yeah. Yeah, that'd be great."

I start to take her hand, but it ends up being a hug. Then I do take her hand, and I lead her around to the passenger side. I open the door for her.

"But, Jennifer," I say when we're both inside. "There's something I need to tell you."